Betting on the Bull Rider

Betting on the Bull Rider

An Elliotts of Montana Romance

Kaylie Newell

TULE
PUBLISHING

Chapter One

ALICE BLOOM STRAIGHTENED the colorful flower arrangement that sat in the bay window of the Victorian house that had been in her family for three generations. Well, four now. Counting her.

The Montana sun filled the sitting room with golden, summer light. The house was warm, but not too warm. She didn't want the family and friends of Mrs. Elaine Chapman to be uncomfortable in any way. Alice's dad had a tendency to turn up the air conditioning until people's teeth started chattering. *Nobody wants to stick to their chair during a funeral!* he'd say. But nobody wanted to freeze to death at one, either.

The door to the basement squeaked open behind her, and she turned to see Dana standing there in her signature black slacks and matching sweater. It didn't matter that Dana was the embalmer, and dealt with the dead for a living. She wore black on her days off, too—in the mornings, at night, on the weekends, on vacation…you name it. Alice had even seen her in pictures at Disneyland wearing black jeans and sneakers. Her nose, lip, and eyebrow rings, in sharp contrast to the giant Mickey Mouse emblazoned on her T-shirt. Black, of course.

The younger woman looked around and smiled. "It looks pretty. Nice job, Alice."

"You don't think it's too much? She liked pink."

Mrs. Chapman's family had asked Alice to take care of the flowers, so she'd admittedly gone a little nuts. Pink roses and carnations from Sweet Pea Flowers. Lilies and baby's breath. Everything pink and soft, and painfully feminine. But looking at it now, she wondered if it didn't have more of a Pepto-Bismol vibe going on.

"No, it's cool," Dana said. "It smells like a garden in here."

Good. A garden was good. This funeral might look slightly medicinal, but as long as it didn't smell that way.

Dana walked up beside her and peered out the window, which was open a crack to let some fresh air in. The first of the family members were starting to arrive. A small Volkswagen parked underneath the shade of the big, ancient oak in the yard, acorns crunching underneath its tires. Then a few pickup trucks pulled up behind, lining up like boxcars behind a train.

"Ninety-eight," Dana said. "Passed away in her sleep after an evening spent with her book club? Not a bad way to go, if you ask me."

"Not too shabby." Alice glanced over at her. "Is that new?"

"It's a septum ring," Dana said matter-of-factly. "Your dad is worried that when I take a drink of water, it'll squirt out from all the holes in my head. Like a sprinkler. His exact words."

Alice laughed. "You know he loves you. He's just a little old-fashioned. Progressively old-fashioned. That's my dad."

"I get it. I'm sure my dad would feel the same."

Dana had only been in Marietta for six months. She'd graduated from mortuary sciences school in December, and had answered Bloom Funeral Home's ad for an embalmer right after. Alice had liked her immediately. Even though they were complete opposites, she felt like Dana was the little sister she'd never had. She was protective of her, even though the younger woman could absolutely take care of herself. She rode a vintage Honda dirt bike she'd nicknamed Sugar Bear. So, there was that.

They were still getting to know each other, but it was pretty obvious that Dana and her family were estranged. It made Alice sad. As the only child of a widower, she knew what a gift family could be. How lonely you could feel without it. She also knew how it felt to be an outcast—a square peg trying to fit into a perpetually round hole. Being the weird little kid of a small-town mortician did that to you.

"So, what do you say?" Dana asked, as they watched Mrs. Chapman's family and friends make their way up the flower-lined walkway. "Your birthday is day after tomorrow. The big three-four. Are you going to let me take you to the Wolf Den for tequila shots?"

"God. I was hoping you'd forget about that."

"Never."

"I hate tequila."

"You haven't tried the *right* tequila."

"There is no right tequila."

"Live a little, Alice."

"I've made it this far. I must be doing something right."

Dana sighed. "By washing your hands fifty times a day?"

"What are we talking about?"

They both turned to see Alice's dad, looking dapper in his black suit and tie. His snow-white hair was combed neatly over an endearing bald spot, and a soft paunch hung over his belt buckle.

"I'm trying to get Alice to loosen up for her birthday, Mr. Bloom," Dana said. "It's a losing battle."

"She won't do it, Dana, my dear. I've tried."

Alice crossed her arms over her chest, feeling the cool weight of her mother's pearls against her throat. "Well, now you're just making me sound like a prude."

He leaned over and gave her a kiss on the cheek, something that always melted her pretend defenses. Alice had only ever been truly mad at her father twice in her life. Once when he'd washed her favorite blue dress in hot water and shrunk it three sizes. And that time he'd forgotten to mention that her mom was dying.

"Here they are," Dana said. And her pretty, pierced face transformed into something exquisite as she smiled at the first of the Chapman family to walk through the door.

Alice smiled, too. Stepping forward to shake their hands and extend her warmest condolences. Nobody ever really understood this, but she loved it. Not the death part, of course. But the comforting part. She got how it felt to lose someone. What it was like to say goodbye in a flower-filled room with tissues on every table. These families with the red noses and sad eyes were her people. And there was a special place in her heart for each and every one.

People filed past, making their way into the light-filled mortuary that smelled like rose petals. The house was lovely, in and of itself. But it also exuded a quiet kind of dignity, of old beauty that was hard to explain until you stepped foot inside its walls. It smelled like summer. But it felt like summer, too.

Alice glanced down the line of people coming up the walkway. There were a few elderly folks slapping their canes on the cement, or leaning on a walker or two. But most of them were young—nieces, nephews, friends. Overall, this group of people didn't look so much solemn, as ready to celebrate the woman they'd come to honor. Mrs. Chapman had lived a good life, a long life, and as far as funerals went, this was about as peaceful as you could hope for.

The last of the guests walked through the door—a middle-aged man and a little girl of about five or so. She wore a ruffled dress and a crooked bow in her hair, and clutched the man's hand like it was a life preserver.

Bending down, Alice touched her puffy sleeve. "Hello there. I like your dress."

The girl's eyes were so blue, they looked almost periwinkle. "Thank you."

Alice smiled. "There are still plenty of seats toward the back. Thank you so much for coming."

The man led the little girl into the other room where the pianist had started playing *A Closer Walk to Thee.*

"I think that's it," Dana said softly.

"Okay. I'll be right there."

She started pushing the front door closed against the warmth of the morning, when a big, black truck rumbled up to the curb. It was so huge that the driver had to park with its tail end jutting into the road.

Alice frowned disapprovingly. Maybe she was a prude. But at least she didn't block the street during a funeral.

The door opened and a man in a white Stetson climbed out. He slammed the door and walked around the front of his truck, obviously in a hurry. Then stopped and touched his hat, as if he'd forgotten it was still there.

Alice watched as he turned around, opened the door again and swiped the hat off his head to toss it in the driver's seat. He ran his hand through his strawberry blond hair, doing nothing to erase the hat ring. He wore a denim shirt, dark-washed Wranglers, and boots. The boots were worn, dusty. His belt buckle giant and gleaming in the sun. She'd didn't hang out with any personally, but she'd seen enough cowboys around Marietta to know this guy was the real deal. The Wranglers might be new, but the boots weren't. And that said a lot.

He headed up the walkway, oblivious to her standing there. All of a sudden, she felt awkward, like she'd been waiting for him. Which, she guessed she had been.

She swallowed hard. It was absolutely not the time or place to be noticing how his shirt stretched over his broad shoulders. And despite the five-o'clock shadow at ten o'clock in the morning, he also looked about a decade younger than her, which only made her feel more awkward, if that was possible.

She plastered a smile on her face, and waited for him to reach the front steps. Sometimes this happened. A bolt of desire would hit like a lightning rod out of a clear blue sky. Then she'd have to remind herself that tall cowboys with hat rings around their hair didn't notice her. They ignored her. And that was okay, because the pain of her childhood was in the rearview mirror now, and she was happy with the woman she was. She was a helper, a comforter. And despite how boring Dana thought her life was, she was good with it.

He took the steps two at a time, and then stomped his boots on the porch, ridding them of some dirt. She waited until he looked up and saw her standing there.

"Hello," she said. Softly, in her best funeral director's voice. It no longer mattered that he'd parked his truck crooked, or that he smelled faintly of soap and man. Or that she'd spent the better part of her teens crying over guys just like this. He was here to say goodbye to someone, and she was going to help him do that.

He nodded. Then smiled, and touched the brim of his hat, which at this very moment sat in the driver's seat of his pickup.

"Ma'am. I'm a little late."

"That's okay. They haven't started yet."

He walked over, dwarfing her in his presence. Then reached out to shake her hand. "Jake Elliott. A neighbor of Elaine's."

Her fingers disappeared underneath his. His skin was

rough and warm, his movements measured, confident. His face was tan, and thin white lines made their way from the corners of his hazel eyes. A twenty-something's version of crow's feet. She, on the other hand, had the beginnings of the real thing.

"Alice Bloom," she said. "I'm so sorry for your loss."

"Thank you." He looked toward the room where the reverend was now at the podium straightening her notes and clearing her throat.

Without another word, Jake Elliott walked into the chapel with his head bowed. His broad shoulders rounded. He looked too big for the room, and Alice watched him go, her heart beating steadily behind her breastbone. Men like that looked too big for everything.

"Alice!" her dad whispered from the doorway.

She looked over, pulled back into a reality she'd momentarily forgotten.

"Turn up the air," he said. "It's warm in here."

Chapter Two

J AKE TOSSED THE whiskey back, and it burned like a lit
match going down. He should really quit. The room was
starting to spin, but it had been a hell of a day, and the news
from his physical therapist had cemented his current mood.

The music from the jukebox pulsed through the Wolf
Den with a deep, electric urgency. The bar was crowded, but
it usually was on Saturday nights. The country songs, the
alcohol, the people, all felt as familiar to Jake as a worn pair
of jeans. The only thing different about tonight was the fact
that he'd usually have a curvy blonde on his arm. The kind
of woman who'd only be too happy to lick his wounds.
Buckle bunnies. That's what everyone called them. Girls who
followed cowboys around on the circuit, looking for love in
all the wrong places. Or all the right places, depending on
who you were talking to.

The bartender looked at him questioningly, and Jake
shook his head. He was done for the night. He'd ridden the
Harley, but at this rate, Jesse would have to give him a ride
back to his place, which he wasn't looking forward to. Jake
hated depending on anyone for anything. Even a lift.

He scanned the room for his brother now, and found

him standing next to the pool table with a couple of women hanging all over him. He was laughing, oozing the characteristic Elliott charm. They all had it, or so he'd been told. Although he was a little rougher around the edges than his brothers. You kind of had to be when you rode bulls for a living.

Jake ran a hand through his hair, wincing at the pain in his shoulder. Scratch that. Maybe he *used* to ride bulls for a living. That is, if he couldn't get this damn thing healed up by the Copper Mountain Rodeo. He was twenty-eight. And that was approaching geezerville as far as bull riders went. Twenty-eight, and his body was already giving out on him. He walked with a limp first thing in the morning, moved stiffly the rest of the day. And lately his knee could tell him with pinpoint accuracy when it was going to rain. But he didn't care. He loved the crazy lifestyle. And so much of his identity was wrapped up in it, he really couldn't see himself doing anything else. Which was dumb. Of course he'd have to do something else. Eventually.

He ran his thumb along the smooth lip of the shot glass, breathing in the smell of sweat and cologne. Of perfume and stale cigarettes. Being a cowboy was all he knew. All he wanted to know. Deep down, he felt the weight of impending change starting to steal his breath. It was like an elephant taking a seat right on his chest, and he wanted to push back with all his strength. Screw getting older. Screw dislocated shoulders and physical therapists who insinuated his joints weren't what they used to be.

Maybe he'd have another drink after all.

People crowded around him at the bar, and someone elbowed him in the ribs, before muttering a drunken apology.

Shifting on his barstool, he leaned away to make room. The bartender pointed at someone behind him.

"What'll it be?"

"Two shots of tequila, please."

The bartender cupped his ear, looking slightly annoyed. "You gotta speak up. Can't hear over the music."

"Two tequila shots?"

Jake rubbed his eyes without looking over. Christ. This lady sounded like a sixteen-year-old at church camp.

"Salt and lime?" the bartender asked. "Or neat?"

The was a pause. "What does neat mean?"

A few people laughed, and the bartender shook his head condescendingly.

The skin on the back of Jake's neck prickled. Okay, so she didn't know how to order tequila. That wasn't any crime, last he checked. But by the sound of it, she'd definitely need help throwing it back.

He leaned toward the sound of her voice without taking his eyes off the bartender. A subtle warning. "Salt and lime," he told her. "Trust me."

Another pause. "Thank you. Salt and lime, please."

"'Atta girl."

"I think I know you?"

Here we go... The pickup lines. He'd heard them all. This wasn't the most original, granted, but he had to give her points for delivery. The tequila thing was pretty adorable.

Shifting on his barstool again, he turned toward the woman whose voice reminded him of a dove's coo. All softness and light. Something he'd accidentally break if given the chance.

She seemed vaguely familiar. Thin, but not skinny. Pale, like she didn't get out much. Hair as black as the midnight sky stretched over Marietta, and the greenest eyes he thought he'd ever seen up close.

She smiled, looking uncomfortable. Like she wanted to bolt. But she lifted her chin slightly, like she was used to fighting that particular urge.

"Jake Elliott?"

He blinked, trying to remember where he knew her from. She definitely didn't run in his circle. Her clothes told him that much. She wore a white blouse buttoned nearly to her chin, and small pearl earrings. She looked like someone who could do his taxes.

Her smile fell a little as the awkwardness grew. Damn it. He felt like he was hurting her feelings, which he probably was. But he honestly couldn't place her. The whiskey wasn't helping.

"I'm sorry…"

"Alice Bloom," she said. "Bloom Funeral Home. You came in the other day for Mrs. Chapman's service?"

Someone pushed her from behind and her thigh rubbed against his knee. Her eyes widened as if he'd just taken one of her earlobes between his teeth.

The recognition settled slowly. *Yeah…* He remembered now. This was the lady at the door. She'd been so proper that he'd tucked her away like a footnote.

She stood here now, watching him, breaking his heart a little in that uptight blouse and hair that caught the bar's neon light like a mink's hide. She'd dressed up for this. For a night at the Wolf Den. Where it wasn't uncommon for people to get sick in the alleyway, and come back in for another game of pool. All of a sudden, he wanted to take her by the elbow and lead her into a quiet corner, where she wouldn't get jostled.

He nodded. "Yeah, I remember. Sorry, that was a long day."

"My condolences about Mrs. Chapman. Elaine."

"Thanks. She was a nice lady."

"Two tequila shots!" the bartender shouted over the jukebox. He slid the drinks over on a small tray with the lime on the side.

"Oh," she said, taking her gaze from Jake's. "Thank you." Reaching into her purse, she pulled out a twenty, and put it on the bar. Then picked up the tray just as someone pushed up behind her to order a beer. The tequila sloshed over the side of the shot glasses, and she bit her bottom lip in concentration. She'd almost been wearing it.

"Can I carry that for you?" Jake asked.

The fact that she might be here with another guy who might not appreciate his chivalry, however innocent, hadn't occurred to him until now. Jake always acted first, thought later. It was why he was such a good bull rider. As far as he was concerned, overthinking anything was the kiss of death. Women, rodeo. You name it.

She smiled, and she actually had a beautiful smile. It transformed her guarded, slightly wizened expression into something very different. It was like watching a moth unfold its wings.

"That's okay. You'll lose your barstool if you get up. My friend…" She scanned the packed room for whoever she'd come with, and all of a sudden he found himself hoping it wasn't another guy. But then the thought skittered away before it could sink its teeth in. She looked married. Or divorced. Probably with two point five kids and a Golden Retriever. Definitely not his type. Still, he found himself looking at that top button of her blouse, and before he could help it, imagined himself undoing it with his clumsy fingers that were too big and rough for something so delicate.

Her gaze settled on someone over at the pool table, and he followed it. Standing there, surrounded by a group of tough-looking cowboys, was an even tougher-looking girl who, unlike Alice Bloom, he recognized immediately. She'd been at the funeral home that day, too. He remembered because she'd been so nice. Also because she had so much metal in her young face. But, hey. To each her own.

"Your friend?" he finished for her. "Looks like she's about to break that eight ball."

Her brows furrowed. There was that worried look again. Like she'd been caught impersonating a police officer.

"I told her to play while I got the drinks. She loves pool. I'm sure she won't be long."

As if on cue, the other woman caught Alice's eye, smiled, and held up a finger, as if to say she'd be just a second. Jake knew better. These kinds of games took a while. Especially if there was money on them, which, if by the looks of those guys was any indication, there was.

He turned back to her with an honest question teetering on the edge of his tongue. *What's a nice girl like you doing in a place like this?*

Someone bumped her again, and her shoulders stiffened as more tequila sloshed over the sides of the shot glasses.

"I don't mind losing my stool," Jake said, standing. "I'm ready to leave, anyway."

She looked up at him, obviously hesitant. Maybe she thought he was going to murder her. Death by tequila shot. Or worse, try and sell her some insurance. Whatever the reason, she was a tough nut to crack, and Jake liked a challenge.

He reached for the tray. "Please?"

She watched him for another few seconds, and something crackled between them that he hadn't been expecting. It was a strong undercurrent, something raw and a little jolting.

Her gaze dropped to his outstretched hand. Then she handed the tray over. "Thank you."

"Do you have a table?"

"Over there."

Holding the tray, he pushed his way through the crowd, making sure to create a swath big enough for her to follow without being trampled. The place was getting wild.

When he got to the table across the room, he felt like he could breathe again. It was even cooler over here, without all the bodies crammed next to each other at the bar.

He set the tray down and glanced over at her. She was standing there looking more out of place than ever. Her friend was playing pool, and she was all alone. Dressed up and alone, and looking like she'd been stood up for her own prom. He couldn't leave her. Every single red-blooded male cell in his body screamed against it. And, yeah. Maybe she didn't want the company, but he sure as hell was going to try.

She smiled. As if she knew exactly what had crossed his brain just now. "I don't usually go out like this," she said. "I'm a homebody. But it's my birthday, and Dana wanted to go out for drinks, so here we are."

It was her birthday… So that explained a lot. Mainly the expression on her face that said she wanted to be having a good time. She really did, but she was also expecting a zombie apocalypse.

Without thinking, he pulled a chair out for her. She nodded and sat, staring at the tequila shots miserably.

It occurred to him then, that maybe he should leave. Maybe he should get his ass out the door, but not because he was honestly getting a little drunk, and had a headache coming on. Or that he was just plain sick of the bar. But more because as he looked down at her dark hair, he felt himself wanting to reach out and touch it.

He tugged a chair over anyway. "Mind if I sit?"

She looked surprised. And then her pale cheeks flooded with color. "You don't have to feel bad for me," she said, with a little more juice in her voice than he'd come to expect, since he'd known her a whole five minutes. "I'm fine. But thank you."

"Oh, I know you're fine." He winked and there it was. The old Elliott charm had slipped out without even trying. Okay, maybe with a side of Elliott cheese too, but whatever. If it worked, so be it.

"Are you sure?" she asked.

"I'm sure."

She seemed to weigh this. Talk to him for a while, or run in the other direction. "Okay," she finally said.

He felt a small rush of relief, which he wasn't used to. He didn't usually have to work this hard. Usually, he didn't have to work at all.

Sitting, he stretched his legs out in front of him. Her gaze flickered down, and caught for a second on the bulge in his jeans. *Well, now.* This woman was full of surprises.

Her cheeks were now scarlet.

He cleared his throat and handed her a shot glass. "So, it's your birthday?"

"It is."

"How old are you, Alice Bloom?"

"Thirty-four." Her green eyes settled on him with a quiet knowledge. A teacher schooling her student. "How old are you, Jake Elliott?"

"Twenty-eight. But I'm very mature for my age."

She laughed, taking the shot glass, and brushing his fingers with hers.

"Do you like tequila, Alice Bloom?"

"No. I've never had a full shot of it before."

"Well, I'm not going to ask the obvious question of why you're not drinking something else then, and just warn you that tequila shots on your birthday can be a bit dangerous, as I'm sure you already know."

"Danger is my middle name." She said this ironically, with a sparkle in her eyes.

He looked at her blouse, making sure it didn't look like he was trying to look *through* it, which wasn't his fault, because it was kind of sheer, and he could make out the hint of her bra underneath.

"Somehow I doubt that."

"Why's that?"

"The buttons to your chin say otherwise. How long have you worked in a funeral home, Alice?"

"Since college, but I've lived there since birth. It's been in our family for a long time."

"Interesting."

Her lips tilted, and he noticed then that they were plump and very kissable. She wasn't fazed by his Elliott charm and other alpha-male bullshit. She seemed like she wanted to go toe to toe, which he was down for. He could feel his headache easing from his temples by the second.

"What do you do for a living, Jake Elliott?"

He liked how his name sounded coming from those lips. She was bewitching him. Which was weird, since she didn't exactly look like a temptress. In fact, the look he was getting from Jesse right that minute from across the bar was a very curious one.

"I'm a bull rider," he said.

Her eyes widened. "You…"

"Ride bulls."

"At rodeos?"

He smiled. "Traditionally."

"Here? At Copper Mountain?"

"That's the plan. As long as my shoulder holds out. I'm on hiatus at the moment, until my physical therapist says I'm good to go."

She frowned. "You've been hurt."

"It happens."

"It's dangerous."

"Yes. Does that bother you?"

"I lied…danger isn't my middle name."

"Bingo."

She stared at the shot glass in her hand as if it had suddenly caught fire.

"I think it's time to toss that back," he said. "Before you lose your nerve."

"Who said I had any nerve?"

"Me. I lied, too. I can see it."

"You don't know me very well."

He picked up the other shot of tequila. "I'll buy your friend another. I'm going to do this one with you. Teach you how. Cool?"

She contemplated that for a few seconds. Then nodded. "Okay. But I have to warn you, I might spit it out all over you."

"You won't. It'll be fine."

She didn't look convinced.

"Okay," he said. "The salt's on the rim, so that's easy. One less step. The trick is to throw it back fast. Swallow, then suck." He held up the lime for a visual aid.

"Swallow, then suck," she repeated, like she was repeating directions on how to fix her carburetor.

"Ready?"

"No. It smells disgusting."

"Don't smell it. Ready?"

She nodded, looking him straight in the eyes. She was honestly scared of taking a shot. What other wonders could Alice Bloom be taught with a guy like him leading the way? Before he could help it, his mind descended directly into the gutter, but that wasn't a surprise. That's where it had a tendency to stay.

"Happy birthday, Alice Bloom," he said. "One, two…"

She watched him as the music pulsed through the bar. As the crowd pulsed around them. As his blood pulsed through his veins.

"Three," he said.

They both brought the tequila to their lips in unison. He slammed his back, never taking his gaze off her. She screwed up her face and tilted her head back, swallowing in one giant gulp.

"Suck!"

Before she could start coughing, he pressed his lime to her mouth, since she seemed to have forgotten she had one of her own.

She bit into the fat, green slice with her eyes still shut, a look of pure disgust on her face. He laughed. He couldn't help it.

Then she did cough. She coughed and sputtered, enough to make a few people look over, but she'd swallowed it down like a champ. All that was left of her birthday tequila was a wilty-looking lime wedge and an empty glass. Just as it should be.

He reached over and turned the glass upside down on the table, then slapped her shoulder triumphantly. "You did it."

She opened her eyes. "That was…"

"An adventure?"

"Awful."

"But you did it."

Her lips stretched into a smile. "I did it."

Sitting back in his chair, he rubbed his jaw, which was thick with stubble. "Can I ask why it took thirty-four years though? That seems excessive."

"No, it's okay. It is excessive."

He waited. She pushed the tray away, as if it'd grow another tequila shot on it like a blackberry weed.

"In a nutshell?" she said.

"Sure."

"I'm scared of everything."

She watched him for a reaction, and he made sure not to say something offensive, like *you look it.* She did look it. But he hadn't been lying earlier when he'd said he could see her nerve, too.

Instead, he rubbed his hands down his thighs. "Why?" he asked simply.

She laughed. "There's not enough time to tell you."

"Try me."

She pulled her bottom lip between her teeth, something he had to work hard not to stare at.

Taking a deep breath, she leaned forward with her elbows on the table. Her silky hair fell forward, partially covering one eye before she pushed it back again. "Well, my mom died when I was little. I grew up in a funeral home around dead people. Around death in general. I saw my mom in everyone and everything. It was like the movie *My Girl*. Have you seen it?"

"Is that the one where her friend gets stung by the bees?" He vaguely remembered watching it on cable once when the PBR coverage had ended for the night. His eyes had gotten misty and he'd turned it off. "It was terrible."

"No it wasn't!" She looked genuinely appalled.

"Okay. Go on."

"Well, it was like that movie in that I struggled with fear from the beginning. That could happen to me...what if it *does* happen to me? That kind of thing. Then the fear turned into anxiety, the anxiety into germophobia, so on and so forth." She shrugged.

"I'm sorry about your mom."

"Thanks."

"What are you afraid of? Specifically."

"Oh, God. You don't want to know."

He did want to know. In fact, he found himself wanting to learn as much as he possibly could about this woman before she got up and walked out of his life forever. He could almost see her as a skinny little kid, surrounded by caskets and flowers and leather-bound condolence books. It was a strange way to grow up.

He leaned forward and put his elbows on the table, too. Their faces were so close now that he could see the fine lines around her eyes. They were an imperfection that weren't really an imperfection at all.

"Tell me," he said.

Someone smacked the pool balls across the room. The people standing around the table let out a collective *ahh,* and she glanced over before looking back at him again.

"Choking, for one."

He raised his brows. "Choking."

"I had a friend who needed the Heimlich once. French toast. I never got over it."

"Okay. Choking. What else."

"Flying…heights, getting old, not getting old, norovirus, influenza, spiders, car accidents, dogs, spinal injuries, and brain-eating amoebas."

She stared at him.

He had to put a hand over his mouth to keep from smiling. When he'd schooled his expression, he took it away again.

"You're a hot mess, Alice."

"I know."

"Brain-eating amoebas?"

"I forgot skinny-dipping."

"Of course you did."

"It's a general fear of getting naked and getting caught. Plus, you could also contract brain-eating amoebas *while* skinny-dipping, so. There's that."

She was joking now. It was possible the tequila was starting to have a nice effect. One more shot and she might get even more interesting, and that was dangerous. He'd warned her.

"Have you ever tried skinny-dipping?" he asked.

"Uh, no."

"Miracle Lake has a nice little cove. Pretty secluded. I could take you out there sometime."

"What?" She laughed. "No way."

"I'm just saying."

"What about you, anyway?"

"I've tried it. And liked it."

"No, I mean what about you? Why are you a bull rider?"

He ran a hand through his hair. He was used to people asking. Like her, he did something for a living that interested them. Something not everyone could wrap their mind around. He had a standard answer. *I'm an adrenaline junkie.* Which was true, but it didn't quite cut to the marrow like he knew she wanted. The biggest reason he rode bulls was something he was still coming to grips with himself. And he didn't know that he could admit anything to a woman he'd just met and was trying his damnedest not to scare off at the moment.

"I grew up on a farm," he said. "Sleigh Bell, you might know it."

"Yeah…I think I do. Out on the highway. It's beautiful."

He nodded. "I was raised around large animals. I have three brothers, so it didn't take long to start daring each other to see how long we could stay on. That kind of thing. I caught the rodeo bug early, to my mom's dismay. And my dad's too, I guess. But I make a decent living and put most of it away, so they can't complain too much."

"But I'm sure they worry about you…"

She said that part with a frown, studying him like some newly discovered swamp species.

"Oh, yeah. They worry. That's natural."

"And do you ever worry about yourself?"

"I think about the possibility of getting hurt, sure. But the thrill outweighs all that. All part of being a cowboy." He winked.

She wasn't impressed.

"I think it's reckless," she said.

He sat back. Feisty. She wasn't going to beat around the bush here.

"Tell me what you really think."

"I'm sorry. None of my business."

"You don't think it's a little sexy? The cowboy thing?" He grinned.

This time, she grinned too, and looked down at her hands for a second. The old Elliott charm was in overdrive tonight.

When she looked back up, her eyes were sparkling. "You don't seem to suffer from a lack of confidence."

"Well, no."

"And the cowboy thing works for you? With women?"

"I do all right."

"And they're okay with the reckless part?"

No, they weren't. At least not the ones who'd really come to mean something to him. His first serious girlfriend, a girl named Becky with long brown hair and freckles, had told him she couldn't keep holding her breath every Saturday night. She had a chubby baby now, and a husband who practiced law on the outskirts of town. He still thought about her sometimes.

Alice smiled, but it was sad-looking. As if his silence was all the answer she'd needed. "I just see too much death, I guess," she said. "Life is too precious to gamble away."

He nodded. He could understand why she felt that way. A lot of people felt that way. He loved what he did, but he wasn't stupid. He understood the risks.

"Don't you ever want to slow down?" she continued. "Stop and smell the roses?"

He considered this. "Sounds boring."

"It's not, though. A walk through a park. Or browsing through a bookstore on a rainy day. Or dressing up to go to the opera… Have you ever been to the opera?"

He watched her.

"Okay," she said with a laugh. "But I bet you'd like it if you ever went."

"I bet you'd like skinny-dipping if you ever went."

She shook her head and ran a finger around the base of the empty shot glass, her expression shuttered. *No way. Case closed. End of report.* Only thing was, Jake didn't take too well to anyone telling him something was impossible. Everything was possible. Even getting this woman out of her business attire and into a freezing-ass lake in July was possible. Theoretically.

He felt the corners of his mouth tug into a smile. And this time it had nothing to do with trying to charm her. And had everything to do with a challenge that had presented itself like a shiny new bike on Christmas morning.

"Hey, Alice Bloom," he said. "How would you feel about a friendly wager?"

Chapter Three

"YOU DID *WHAT?*"

Dana stared at her over the casket catalogs that were spread out over the polished, cherrywood table. Alice straightened them carefully. If she wasn't in the funeral home business, she'd never believe how many choices there were for the picky consumer. Caskets were like cars. There was one for every personality.

"It was just a silly bet. I'm sure I'll never see him again."

"Wait, wait." Dana held up a hand and closed her eyes, momentarily processing this. "The guy from Mrs. Chapman's service?" She opened her eyes again and stared at her. "The cowboy?"

Alice nodded. *The one and only.* She hadn't been able to believe it herself when she'd come up behind him at the bar the other night. But the shoulders were the same. The hair that begged to have a woman's hands running through it. The strong profile that reminded her of something in an old western. The same guy. Her ovaries had recognized him before she had.

"Well." Dana crossed her arms over her chest, and smiled. The line of diamond studs marching up each earlobe twinkled. "I need to leave you alone to play pool more often."

The old house smelled like lemon this morning. The hardwood floors gleamed, reflecting the light from the vintage lamps on the end tables. The delicate chandelier in the entryway sparkled, sending rainbow prisms bouncing off the walls. It was the kind of day she loved. Death was part of the job. But there was a peacefulness in this house that she'd always had a hard time explaining to other people.

"I saw you two talking," Dana continued. "So I figured you wouldn't mind if I finished the game…"

Alice's cheeks heated. Dana's pool playing had been just fine. In fact, she was mildly surprised the table separating her and Jake Elliott hadn't caught fire from all the sparks flying between them. Never in her life had she experienced such pure attraction. It had taken her off guard. More than that. It had swept her off her feet.

But Alice was a realist, and she knew the tequila probably had something to do with that. The time of night, their surroundings. It was all like blowing on kindling. And as drawn as she'd been to him, she knew the chances of hearing from him again were slim to none. He was the kind of man who lived his life on the precipice.

She glanced down at her gray silk blouse and sensible black skirt. She was not what you'd call the precipice type.

"But I digress," Dana said. "What kind of bet?"

"Oh…something about opera and skinny-dipping."

"*Alice!*" Dana looked delighted.

"I told you it was silly."

"I'm here to tell you, there's nothing silly about skinny-dipping."

"You've been?"

"Of course I've been." Dana waved her hand in an all-encompassing arc. "There are so many places around here. The lake, the river…"

"All at hypothermic temperatures, I'm sure."

"That's why it's call dipping, Alice. Not marinating."

Alice laughed. It was ridiculous. But there was a definite brush of butterflies against her rib cage at the memory of making that bet. Which seemed so long ago now.

"It doesn't matter," she said. "It was just the tequila talking, anyway."

"Good morning, ladies!"

Alice's dad appeared in the doorway, looking starched and pressed, as usual. He held a Bloom Funeral Home mug that contained his morning coffee. Alice had ordered a box of them on a whim a few years ago, and now she couldn't remember what she'd been thinking at the time. Nobody wanted to drink their coffee in a funeral home mug. Except maybe a funeral home director.

She gave Dana a *zip it* look, and Dana gazed back, unfazed. Her father would not understand a skinny-dipping bet made with a local rodeo star.

"We've got the Gilchrist service at four," he said, looking at his watch with the worn leather band. It didn't match his black suits, or his shining shoes. But it had been a gift from his wife, so he wore it faithfully every day.

"The flowers will be here at three," Alice said. "Lilies, her favorite. It's going to be just lovely."

Dana nodded. "We're right on track, Mr. Bloom."

"Good, good. We'll give her a nice send-off, won't we?"

Josephine Gilchrist had lived at May Bell Center until she'd died of heart failure a few days ago. A nurse during World War II, she'd been struggling financially, and had no living relatives. Aside from a few friends, she'd passed alone, something Charles Bloom saw all too often in his line of work. He'd wanted to see to it that Josephine was laid to rest in a way she deserved. Alice was proud of her father. This wasn't the first time he'd held a funeral for a stranger. And it wouldn't be the last.

He brought the steaming mug to his lips and took a sip, eyeing the two women over its rim.

Alice cleared her throat, hoping he wouldn't be able to read the look on her face. Or that he hadn't heard the conversation taking place when he'd walked up. She tried to remember what she'd said last, and if it included the words *skinny*, or *dipping*.

He smiled at them leisurely. Alice smiled back.

"Okay then," he said. "I'll check back in later."

"All right, Mr. Bloom." Dana was thoroughly unaffected. In fact, she seemed to be enjoying the fact that Alice was squirming.

He walked away, and when Alice was sure he wouldn't be able to hear, she turned to her friend. "Dana. You have to promise not to mention this to Dad."

Dana inspected her purple nails. "Why not? He might appreciate it. If anyone can get you to live a little, it's that cowboy, Alice."

"That's exactly what I'm talking about. I don't need anyone to get me to live a little. I'm just fine…not living?" That hadn't come out right.

Dana smiled. "Touché."

"I think Dad would only worry. He usually does. And honestly, you knowing is all I can handle."

"Got it."

"Good. Thank you." Alice walked around the table and prepared to make her exit. She had things to do. Funeraly things.

"Whoa, whoa, whoa," Dana said. "Where do you think you're going?"

"To polish something."

"Yeah, nice try. You need to finish telling me about this bet. Details, please."

Alice considered this. If her young friend didn't have all the facts, she'd just start making stuff up. And honestly, there wasn't that much to tell, anyway. Might as well just spill the beans. What there was of them.

She shrugged, and picked some imaginary lint off her blouse. "We were just talking about, you know. How different we are. The fact that he's a bull rider and I'm a funeral home director…"

"Go on."

"And how I'm a little afraid of things."

Dana raised her brows.

"Okay, a lot afraid."

"Uh-huh…"

"And how he's not really afraid of anything. Kind of like you."

"I like him already."

"And then he bet that he could get me skinny-dipping. But that's crazy, because—"

"I know. Toxic algae."

"Brain-eating amoebas." *Good grief.* She couldn't be the only one who read the articles.

"Okay, *and?*"

"And I bet I could get him to the opera. Can you believe he's never been to the opera?"

"Somehow? Yes."

"That's it. That's the bet. And then he got up and shook my hand."

"Actually, he kissed it. I saw that part."

"He kissed my hand." He *had* kissed it, but that seemed like an intimate detail. "And he left."

"Did you exchange numbers?"

"No. It was just a few minutes of banter. That's it. Besides, he's too young for me."

"Girl, please," Dana sighed, rolling her eyes.

"Well, he is."

"I love this bet. I absolutely love it. There's no reason why you can't march right down to the fairgrounds and start asking around about this guy."

"Are you insane? No."

Dana ignored her. "Actually, you wouldn't even have to go that far. We could start asking around town. I know a few people in that rodeo circle."

"Don't you dare."

"Marietta's a small town. You're bound to run into him eventually."

"Well, that's fine. By then he'll have forgotten all about me."

Dana winked, her dark eyes looking exotic underneath the even darker makeup. "The cougar mortician? As if."

"You're impossible."

"But you love me."

Alice smiled and put her arm around the younger woman, whom she dwarfed by a good three inches. "But I love you."

"Tequila shots this weekend?"

It did sound tempting.

Chapter Four

JAKE WALKED OUT of barn 2B at the Marietta fairgrounds, and into the mud and slop next to the arena. They'd had a late July thunderstorm yesterday that had left the entire county drenched, but cooled off from the recent baking temperatures. It was still overcast, and he was glad. Dark, pregnant clouds hung low over the mountains, hinting at more rain later. The air smelled sweet and fresh, but also sharp with the scent of animals—something he'd always loved.

He'd come out this morning to look at a bull he was interested in buying—a young Brahma cross with strong bloodlines that was in the process of being shipped to a new ranch across the state. He was a beautiful animal. Red as Oklahoma clay—muscled and thick, with a promising rodeo temperament. His name was Buckshot, and when Jake had reached out to touch his course, thick hide, he'd almost been able to see him grazing at his place—a ten-acre spread that had taken him nearly as many years to save for.

But now that he had it, he was finally being forced to look his future in the eyes. It had been weighing on him like Buckshot himself. All fifteen hundred pounds of what the hell am I going to do five years from now? With every shooting pain in his shoulder, it was getting clearer and clearer that he couldn't rodeo forever. Bodies wore out. There was an end to every line.

He walked past the arena, watching a young girl taking her horse around some barrels, and thought about how much he had in savings. A bull like this wouldn't be cheap. And he'd need a nice cow too, as that's how these things usually worked. The ranch had taken up most of his prize money, but he still had some put away. Becoming a stock contractor would be a natural fit a few years down the road. He knew more about these animals than some of the vets he'd met on the circuit. And it was a hell of a lot safer than riding them day in and day out. But damn, he loved rodeo. And he'd probably do it until they carried him out of the arena on a stretcher, if he was being honest with himself.

Jake headed toward his Harley, the muddy water slopping underneath his boots. Probably not the best day for his bike, but he lived close, and he'd never minded getting a little wet. Besides, the air had felt too good against his skin this morning to resist.

Behind him, there was the low drone of semis passing on the highway, gearing up for the long, slow haul up the mountain range. But over that, there was a distinctive *whir* of tires spinning in the mud.

Frowning, he turned. Sure enough, on the other side of the parking lot, was a small Honda Civic struggling to lurch free of a rut in the sludge. The back tires would stop, then spin again, kicking up muddy water and gravel, but doing nothing to move the car itself. It rocked like a turtle on its back.

Jake pushed his Stetson up with his index finger. "What the…"

He could see the silhouette of the driver pounding the steering wheel in frustration. Bad judgment. Everyone around here knew this place flooded after a storm like something out of the Bible. A two-wheel drive didn't stand a chance against these potholes.

Sighing, Jake began walking toward it. Between the two of them, they'd be able to push it out no problem, assuming the driver was able-bodied enough.

The car revved its engine again, as if willpower alone would make the damn thing move.

Jake held up a hand as he came up behind it. "Hold up!" he yelled. "You're just ruining your tires!"

The driver turned toward the sound of his voice.

He could see through the lightly tinted back window that the silhouette was softer now. There was dark hair in a ponytail. He could see that part clearly. And something in his chest tightened.

The driver's side window rolled down, and a long, slender arm popped out to wave him away. "It's okay! I've got it!"

The car revved again, and Jake had to duck to keep from getting hit with a flying glob of mud and horse crap.

"Sorry!"

That voice… That slightly raspy, ultra-feminine voice that held just enough embarrassment to be irresistible. He recognized that voice.

Before she could rev the engine again, this time successfully spraying him with week-old manure, he stepped up to the open window.

"Wait! Just wait a second," he said. "Hold up."

He leaned down to peer into the driver's seat.

There, peering back, was Alice Bloom. Funeral home director extraordinaire.

"What the hell?" he muttered.

"Shoot." She sagged forward and tapped her forehead against the steering wheel.

She looked different today. Not so much like someone who could do his taxes, as maybe someone he could take to a baseball game. She wore jeans and a white T-shirt. Nothing fancy. Her hair was up, away from her face, and he saw now in the light of day, that she had the most translucent skin he thought he'd ever seen. Maybe it was the way it contrasted with her hair. Or her eyes, which were a clearer green than he'd remembered. But whatever the reason, it made him want to reach out and touch her. And this was the second time she'd made him feel that way. *Two for two.*

"What are you doing here?"

She looked up at him. There were two bright spots of color on her cheeks. "Nothing. Taking a drive."

"Through the parking lot of the fairgrounds?"

"Uh…sure."

"Come on."

"I take drives out this way all the time."

That was bullshit and they both knew it. He grinned

slowly, something that he could tell wormed its way under her skin. In response, she settled an aristocratic gaze on him, which was impressive, since she was the one stuck in the mud.

"Well, I do," she said.

"Okay."

He watched her, trying to remember the reason he'd talked himself out of tracking her down after those shots at the bar. *They were too different...* That had been it. Too different, which meant they had nothing in common, which meant the chances of actually getting her out of her clothes and into the icy waters of Miracle Lake were slim to none. But still, he hadn't been able to stop thinking about her and that stupid bet. And standing here now, looking down into her pretty face, he understood why.

"So," he said. "You want some help getting unstuck?"

"Oh..."

He made a show of leaning back to eye her back tire, and shook his head. "I think you're gonna need some help. Whether you want it or not."

The expression on her face seemed to indicate she didn't want it.

Before she could answer, he fixed her with his most pompous, most infuriating stare. He knew it was pompous and infuriating, because an ex-girlfriend had told him so. In fact, she'd slapped him in the back of the head afterward, so he knew she'd been on to something.

"First, though," he said, his voice smooth as scotch. "Want to tell me how you knew I'd be out here this morning?"

Her eyes widened. "What?"

"Me. Out here. This morning. This is just too much of a coincidence, Alice Bloom."

Her cheeks, which had been red a minute ago, deepened to an almost maroon. This was fun.

"I didn't know you were out here!"

"Hey." He shrugged. "I don't mind."

"You're just... You think I followed you?"

"Did you?"

She rolled her eyes so far into her head, he was surprised they didn't get stuck up there.

"No," she said. "I didn't."

"Okay."

"You don't believe me."

"I believe you don't believe yourself."

"What's that supposed to mean?"

"It *means*, it's okay to be drawn to each other, Alice."

Her mouth hung open. She was obviously not a woman who was used to sparring with spurs on. Of course, this was his happy place.

"Who said..."

"I said. You know how I know?"

She waited, looking incredulous.

"Because I found myself near the funeral home this week, too. Just like you're finding yourself near the fairgrounds now. Which, hey. It's a good guess. Everyone knows I'm out here plenty..."

It looked like her head was about to explode. His gaze

dropped to the base of her throat where a tiny blue vein tapped away, trying to keep up. She had a beautiful neck—long and slender, and he imagined it might smell like perfume, even though all he could smell at the moment was impending rain.

A few drops stung the back of his neck, and he squinted, looking up. "It's going to dump soon."

She was still too flustered to answer. She looked like she wanted to kick him directly in the balls. Maybe he should've stopped while he was ahead.

He reached up and pulled his Stetson low over his eyes. Then leaned down and put his hands on his knees. "Look, I'm sorry," he said. "I'm an acquired taste. Will you *please* let me help you get unstuck?"

"Are you going to lord this over me for all eternity?"

"All eternity? No. Until I win that bet? Maybe."

"There's no way I'm going skinny-dipping with you."

"And there's no way I'm going to the opera with you."

Her eyebrows arched at that. She obviously thought she had a chance there. That's fine. He'd let her.

"Tell you what," he continued. "Let's take baby steps, here. I agree. Skinny-dipping is a lot to swallow at first. But so is the opera. So to be fair, we should have a few micro-bets leading up to the mother lode. If I can get you to check off some of the things on your afraid-of list, then I'll check off a few of the things on my boring-as-hell list. Leading up to Miracle Lake in September."

"Or the opera in October."

"Yeah, whatever. The point is, I think we should make

good on this bet. I'm not gonna lie, I'm curious to see what you're capable of."

She stared up at him. She was just fiery enough to bite, he could tell.

"And I'm curious to see what *you're* capable of," she replied evenly.

"Well, if you want to see me out of my comfort zone, i.e. bookstores and crap, then you're going to have to participate."

"In the form of micro-bets?"

"In the form of micro-bets," he said.

They watched each other. An epic stare-down that only two people who were stubborn as mules could accomplish in a fifteen-second time span. It felt like dog years.

The stinging droplets of rain were plumping into fat drops as he stood there. They splashed into the surrounding mud puddles like miniature bombs, while petulant thunder rumbled in the distance.

Alice Bloom blinked and looked up at the sky, deciding how important agreeing to the bet was, versus letting her upholstery get soaked.

He'd make it easy for her. It looked like she was kind of OCD where her car was concerned.

"We can hash the details out later," he said. "If it makes you feel any better."

She nodded, squinting against the rain in her face. "Deal."

"Okay, I'm just going to go back there and rock it a little. See if that'll work."

"What about your shoulder?"

The truth was, his physical therapist would probably have his ass. But he smiled to reassure her. "I'll be careful."

He turned and walked to the back of the car. Then stared down at the offending tire. *Shit.* He wasn't going to have to rock anything. No wonder she was stuck—it was flat as a pancake.

"Alice," he said. "Your tire's flat, darlin'."

She stuck her head out the window and peered back at him. Her ponytail whipped in the wind. "What?"

"Your tire's flat."

"Oh, no. Oh, crap."

"Do you have a spare?"

The expression on her face fell. "Well, I used to…"

He watched her, and she gazed back, raindrops hitting her cheeks. He wasn't going to lecture her about keeping her car up. He just wasn't. He wasn't her husband, or boyfriend, or even a friend. Although, that part seemed a little hard to reconcile now. She wasn't exactly a friend, that was true. But she was damn sure more than an acquaintance. What was the classification of someone you really wanted to see naked, but didn't know yet if they flossed or not?

"I know," she said. "I know. I've been meaning to put one in there. I've just been busy."

Walking back to the driver's side door, he bent down again. "Okay. We've got two choices, here. You can call a tow. But it's Sunday morning, and I have no idea if Ernie's even up yet."

She considered this. Most folks in Marietta knew a tow

on Sundays were a crapshoot, since there was exactly one truck, with a driver who liked to sleep late. More often than not, you had to wait for someone to come over from Bozeman.

"Or," he continued, "you can jump on the back of my bike, and I can give you a lift. It's not that far."

"Your bike?"

"My motorcycle."

Her mouth popped open. "What? No. No way."

"I have a helmet."

"I'd rather wait for Ernie."

He shrugged. "Suit yourself."

His T-shirt was getting wet, on its way to being soaked. It clung to his shoulders, and her gaze kept falling to his chest like it was magnetized.

Grabbing her phone from the console, she looked away, flustered. "I really appreciate you stopping, but you're getting all wet. I'll just call a tow."

He hooked his thumbs in his belt loops. "I'll wait."

"You don't have to do that."

"I know I don't have to, but I'm guessing he won't answer. Then what?"

He saw her mental wheels turning. Either she didn't have anyone to pick her up, which he seriously doubted. Or she secretly wanted to get on the back of his bike. It was possible.

Dialing the number, she kept her gaze carefully averted. She sat with her phone to her ear, and looked into the distance as if she wanted to blend right into the seat.

A good twenty seconds passed. Then thirty. Then he

smiled.

"No answer?"

She kept the phone glued to her ear. "Not yet."

"I wouldn't hold your breath."

Chapter Five

ALICE STOOD A few feet back from the tall man who rode bulls for a living, and who also rode motorcycles for fun, as if she'd be able to protect herself with some good old-fashioned distance. He was a walking death trap.

He was also soaked to the bone. A walking, talking wet T-shirt contest. He'd taken off his white Stetson, and had put it in a bag on the side of the rumbly-looking bike. His hair dripped, and he kept reaching up to slick it back, bringing the T-shirt up to expose a sliver of muscled abdomen. She tried not to stare. But it was getting really, really hard not to.

In fact, she'd been so busy trying to act like he wasn't ringing every single bell she had, that she'd almost forgotten her own wet T-shirt. White. Of course it was. She crossed her arms over her chest self-consciously, but was pretty sure he'd already gotten an eye-full. Her bra was nothing to behold—cotton and pale pink, but it was still a bra, and he was still a guy.

"Here you go," he said, shoving a helmet at her unceremoniously. "It'll be big, but that's okay. It's not—"

"I know. It's not far." He kept saying that. Like they

couldn't get pulverized by a semi right outside the parking lot.

He smiled. "Relax. I've got you."

The words gave her butterflies. She didn't want them giving her butterflies. She didn't want them making her brave when she was feeling like a chicken tender. And she definitely didn't want them making her think there was something between them that there absolutely wasn't. They'd made a bet. Okay, it was kind of a sexy bet. But that was it. And he *was* giving her a ride home. He was soaked, and so was she, and her breasts would be pressed against his back where they'd apparently decided they wanted to be. But that didn't mean anything, either.

Reaching up, she took the elastic band out of her ponytail and shook out her hair so the helmet would fit over it.

He stared at her, and her face heated in the rain. Had that affected him like his sliver of abdomen had affected her? Shaking her hair out? In Alice's experience, shaking one's hair out meant nothing but trying to keep it from getting ratty. But she made a mental note to remember that for later. For…whoever.

"What about you?" she asked.

"I'll be okay."

She doubted that. She had too good of an imagination. She was already picturing him in the road, his head split like a melon. She frowned. This was why there were closed casket funerals.

"Alice." He touched her arm, just briefly, but it was enough to send an electric current throughout her entire body. "It'll be fine. I do this every day."

"In inclement weather?"

"I'm not going to let anything happen to you, okay? Trust me?"

She wanted to. She really did. But it felt like he was talking about more than just getting on the back of his motorcycle, and her heart thumped painfully inside her chest.

Thunder clapped sharply overhead, and she jumped.

"Come on," he said, throwing one long leg over the seat and grabbing the handlebars. He gave her a devilish smile. "Live a little."

He sounded like Dana. She watched him another few seconds. She was freezing, her teeth chattering uncontrollably in her head. But she wasn't quite sure if that had to do with her body temperature, or the thought of wrapping her arms around his mid-section. Probably a little of both.

Pulling in a deep breath, and cursing Ernie the tow truck driver for the tenth time in as many minutes, she reached up and put the helmet over her head. It dropped down on her shoulders like a mop bucket. No wiggling required.

He laughed, starting the engine. The Harley roared to life, and the sound reverberated in her chest. Despite the genuine feeling of dread at the thought of getting on, there was an unmistakable thrill that shot through her, too. It really was a beautiful motorcycle—shiny silver chrome, accentuated by a deep, electric blue paintjob. The rain beaded on its surface like diamonds.

Jake hooked his finger at her, and she stepped forward.

"Climb on, darlin'," he said.

Apparently, he was going to keep calling her that. Which was kind of inconvenient, because it made her want to fall in love with him. He probably called everyone darlin', and as a direct result, half the town was probably in love with him.

Following his example, she threw her leg over the side of the bike, and immediately had to lean into him to keep her balance. Her breasts were delighted, as this was what they'd wanted all along. Her traitorous nipples hardened, and she wondered if he'd be able to feel them right through her bra.

She found the little pegs on either side of the bike for her feet, settled her butt on the seat, and rested her hands awkwardly on his hips.

He reached around and grabbed one hand, pulling her arm all the way around him. "Don't be shy," he said. "You've gotta hang on."

Right. She did need to hang on.

Luckily for her, the hanging on part was very, very pleasant. Doing as she was told, she wrapped her arms around him, this time pressing herself close. The man was hard as granite. Thick and muscular, his body heat defying logic. She felt it soaking into her, warming her. Making her ache in places she never knew existed until now. Her only regret was the stupid helmet, because what she really wanted to do, was lay her cheek against his back, and breathe him in. *Good Lord.* She was in deep here. Really, very deep.

He revved the engine, and the sound rippled through her. She'd never in her life ridden on the back of a Harley. Never had her arms wrapped around a bull rider, or felt her breasts tingle underneath a rain-soaked T-shirt. The feeling was carnal. Was this what it felt like to be a motorcycle babe? Or a motorcycle darlin'?

He turned toward her. "Ready?"

She nodded, but that was dumb, because the helmet was so big, her head just wobbled around inside it. "Ready!" she shouted.

Clutching him for dear life, she felt him kick the stand out from underneath them. His movements were fluid, graceful. Confident, like he'd done this a million times before, which of course, he had. His body slid against hers, his muscles bunching, and her thighs tightened around the backs of his, as he pushed off the ground and accelerated.

The bike lurched forward like an animal, and her heart reacted accordingly. It felt like it was going to beat right out of her chest.

"Hang on!" he shouted over his shoulder.

He couldn't have peeled her off if he'd tried.

JAKE PULLED UP to Bloom Funeral Home with the funeral home director herself perched on the back of his bike. If anyone had told him a few weeks ago that he'd be giving a mortician a lift and liking it, he would've said they were nuts.

Really, for a first-timer, she'd ridden it like a boss. The helmet was too big, of course, and she looked like an ant with it teetering on her slender shoulders, but she'd done it.

She'd stayed put, clutching him around the middle like her life depended on it, which it had. He was proud of her.

Easing the Harley next to the curb, he stuck his boot out to scrape along the cement as they came to a stop. The engine rumbled through the rain, which had lightened to more of a sprinkle. Truth, if she'd waited twenty minutes, she could've walked back, no problem. But he was glad she hadn't. In fact, he found himself wishing the funeral home was in the next county over, so she wouldn't have to unwrap herself from his mid-section so soon. He could actually get used to her hands clasped firmly above his belt buckle, her forearms pressed against his rib cage.

She leaned away, leaving his T-shirt wet and cold against his skin. She was shaking—that was obvious. He could feel her legs quivering against the backs of his.

Holding on to his shoulder to steady herself, she got off the bike. Then reached up to take the helmet off. Her eyes were wide and clear, her cheeks flushed pink. It was possible she'd actually liked it, although he doubted she'd admit that.

He rested one hand on his thigh. "Well, well, well. You didn't die."

"Now it's your turn."

He raised his brows.

"How would you like a behind-the-scenes tour of a funeral home?" she continued. "No holds barred."

"With corpses?"

"*No.* But I'm assuming the house alone makes you uncomfortable. It'd be educational. And as it stands right now, I'm one up on you. I just rode a Harley."

"You did, that's true."

"And you're soaking wet… I could make you a cup of coffee. To thank you for bringing me home," she added quickly.

"All this to get me to the opera?"

"That's the plan."

"I'm *never* going to the opera, Bloom. But I'll come in for a cup of coffee."

She beamed. "I think my dad's home. You can meet him."

"Whoa…"

"Oh, good grief."

"Don't get any ideas. I'm not ready to settle down." He was joking. Kind of.

But even so, he thought she looked a little hurt.

"I'm kidding," he said, softer this time. "Nobody'd want to settle down with me anyway."

She watched him for a few seconds. Maybe letting the words settle. Maybe wondering what the hell she was doing riding on the back of his bike and inviting him in for coffee.

She cocked her head. "Does that mean you're coming inside?"

"Okay," he said, turning off the Harley's engine. "You're right. I've never had a grand tour of a funeral home before. And if I'm going to get you skinny-dipping…"

"No way."

"You keep saying that."

"So do you."

He threw his leg over his bike and stuck his keys in his

pocket. "Okay. Lead the way."

She smiled, as if she'd successfully wrangled him some-how, which he guessed she kind of had. He didn't want to go walking around a creepy funeral parlor, but he didn't want to leave her yet either. And he had to admit he was curious. Curious about what she did. Curious about the old house, which seemed oddly welcoming. Which was weird.

He followed her up the cracked cement walkway, which was lined with red and yellow rosebushes that were exploding in bloom. The house had two large bay windows that looked like big, dark eyes looking out at him. The second story seemed more mysterious, with a softly glowing light in one of the windows. It was a Victorian-era house, baby blue, accentuated in white gingerbread trim. If he was into houses that looked edible, he'd even say it was pretty, since it reminded him of the farmhouse where he grew up. It *was* pretty, it just wasn't his cup of tea. He was into functionali-ty. Easy living. He had one bathroom, and his garage doubled as a weight room.

Alice kept looking over her shoulder as they climbed the porch steps. Probably to make sure he wasn't going to bolt.

"It was built at the start of the 1900s," she said. "It's been in our family for over one hundred years."

"Has it always been a funeral home?" he asked, as she opened the front door. It squeaked on its hinges—a rusty welcome.

"For the most part."

He glanced around. It looked different than the day he'd come for Elaine's funeral. That probably had to do with the fact that it wasn't crammed with flower arrangements. It looked more like a house today. An old house with lots of wood flooring and ancient floral wallpaper. But there was a certain inherent charm that he couldn't deny. After the chill of the ride back, it felt warm and cozy inside. It smelled like there was already coffee brewing in the kitchen, or maybe there had been earlier in the morning.

To his left there was a small sitting room with a desk and a few chairs. Soft, natural light filtered in through the sheer, white curtains. To his right was the chapel where they'd held Elaine's service. It had probably been built as a living room originally, but was big enough to accommodate several dozen people. And straight ahead was a winding staircase with a dark, polished banister. He stood on a plush, red area rug, and suddenly felt like a fish out of water in his old boots and wet T-shirt.

He turned to Alice. "Do you...live here?" He couldn't believe he hadn't asked before. He guessed it hadn't occurred to him that she would, but the place was obviously a business *and* a home. That would've given him the creeps before. But now...now he could almost see it.

Nodding, she smiled. But there was something in her eyes that was guarded. She was watching him closely for any sign of said creeps. And again, he wondered what it must've been like as a kid growing up in a place like this. Not easy. He'd been teased for a childhood lisp. How would he have been treated if he'd lived with dead people in his living room?

"Upstairs," she said. "Do you think that's weird?"

"No. Nope. Not at all."

"You're a terrible liar."

"I'm not lying. That's the weird part."

She shrugged. "I know most folks think...well, you know. My dad moved out after I graduated from college. He wanted me to have the place to myself. He still has his office in the back..."

"But you were raised here?"

"I was. After Mom died, it was just the two of us. It's been the two of us ever since. I think he's worried that it's changed me. Fundamentally. The business of death."

Jake hooked his thumbs in the pockets of his jeans, which were beginning to dry some. "Has it?"

The question felt deep. But only because of the look on her face. Like she might be talking about something she was used to glossing over. Something painful.

"I think there's no way around it," she said quietly. "After a while, it becomes part of your fabric. But I wouldn't change it. I love what I do."

She walked over to the double doors of the chapel, and gazed inside. "This is where the funerals take place," she said. "But you already know that. Some people prefer graveside services, but mostly they're held here. It's easier to control the variables, like temperature and weather. Families already have so much to wrap their arms around. We want to make this part as comfortable as possible."

He looked inside the darkened room. At the podium, and the empty chairs waiting patiently for the bereaved.

"It's an important job," he said. "What you do."

She watched him. He'd never really thought about it before, a mortician's way of life. But he was thinking about it now. How hard it would be to speak to the families, how much they probably needed to be spoken to, to be seen. All of a sudden, he felt a rush of affection toward this woman who was so fundamentally different from him. She lived her life easing people into acceptance. He lived his life running away from it.

"Thanks, Jake," she said.

And he realized it was the first time she'd said his name. Or was it? Maybe it was the first time she'd said it like that. With that unmistakable feeling behind it. It made him uncomfortable. Because he'd felt something, too. Just now. Like a flash of electricity lighting up a dark, overcast sky.

He cleared his throat and stepped away. "And you don't…embalm?"

The question was sudden, jarring, but he needed to say something else. Something to wipe that emotion clean.

She smiled. "No. Dana does that."

"Your pierced friend? She looks twelve." Jesus, his manners had taken a header.

"She's twenty-four. She's really good at her job."

Jake walked over to the staircase and ran his hand along the old, wood banister. It was glossy with new varnish, and smelled like lemon oil. "What makes someone want to be an embalmer, anyway?"

Alice came up next to him. Her hair was drying in soft waves, and he could smell her shampoo, something vaguely fruity. "I can't speak for everyone," she said, "but Dana's interested in the science part. Anatomy. I couldn't do it. I tried. I'm much better with people who are alive. Sometimes it's hard…"

He watched her. A silence fell between them as she looked down at her tennis shoes like they were the most interesting things in the world.

"Hey," he said, touching her elbow. "Hey…"

After a few seconds, she looked up, but she wouldn't meet his eyes. It was obvious she was trying to keep her composure. "Sorry."

"Are you okay?" He was officially out of his depth here, and he knew it. She probably knew it too, but she was a trouper and wasn't letting on.

Jake didn't usually ask that question. Of anyone. It wasn't that he didn't care. Actually, it was the opposite. He was worried he'd start to care too much. He had some experience with naked vulnerability, years and years ago, and it had nearly done him in.

Alice rubbed a finger underneath her nose and sniffed. "I'm fine. It's just that some of this stuff…it can get pretty heavy."

Heavy. And here she was, shouldering the load. He wondered if she ever needed to talk about it. Did she have any friends who wanted to listen to her day that included anecdotes of funerals and embalmings and broken family members? He had a hard time believing people would be standing in line for that.

"I'm curious how you handle all this," he said. "How did you handle it growing up?"

Her gaze shifted to meet his. She looked a little hesitant. Like she didn't really trust this. Hell, *he* didn't trust it. He still couldn't believe he'd ended up here this morning, standing across from his quirky, dark angel from the bar the other night. The one he'd decided not to pursue because this one had been just different enough to give him pause.

"Well, I was an outcast," she said. "Teased a lot. Of course."

"Kids can be shitheads," he said matter-of-factly.

"True."

"But you grew up, you have a successful career. You went into the family business, which I'm sure your dad's pretty happy about. My dad would've been thrilled if I'd followed in his footsteps."

"And what are those?"

"He's a vet."

She crossed her arms over her chest. A big, old grandfather clocked ticked away in the other room. The sound fit. Like they'd been transported back to the start of the 1900s when this place was just a speck of wood on prairie grass. He half expected a maid to walk through the door carrying a tea service for two.

"Why do you ride bulls, Jake?" she asked. "I mean, really."

"I told you. I'm an adrenaline junkie."

"Don't you care about your life?"

"Of course I care about my life."

"But you do something that puts it in jeopardy every day."

Uh-oh. They were getting into girlfriend territory, here. This was about the time Jake slapped his knee, got up and said: it's not you, it's me.

Subconsciously, or maybe consciously, he took a few steps backwards. Toward the door.

She smiled. "I'm lecturing you, aren't I?"

"Uhh…"

"I'm sorry. I didn't mean to. It's just that I have a hard time understanding it. Probably because of my job. Most people try and avoid death."

"Well, I can tell you I don't *want* to die."

"That's a relief."

"And part of the reason you don't understand, is because you haven't done a whole lot of things like ride bulls, right? I mean, that's fair to say?"

"It's fair. But if that's the case, I'll never get it."

"You don't have to ride a bull to understand. Skinny-dipping's a pretty good start."

She smiled, but then it faded on her lips. "Why do you want to take me skinny-dipping so badly?"

"Why do you want to get me to the opera?"

"Easy. So I can see your face when you fall in love with something you weren't expecting."

He hadn't been expecting her. That's for damn sure.

"Well," he said quietly. "There you go."

The room was still. Except for the sound of the grandfather clock ticking, you could hear a pin drop. Alice chewed on the inside of her cheek, her bottom lip plumping out some. He didn't want to notice that so much, but he did.

"Can I ask you one more question?" she said.

They hadn't had coffee yet. In fact, in the last few minutes, he'd forgotten the coffee all together. He'd forgotten that this was where dead bodies had their hair done, and where gaudy flower arrangements came to die. All he really cared about was the woman standing in front of him, and what was going through her head right that second. He couldn't remember the last time someone had captivated him this much. And he couldn't decide how he felt about that.

"Sure," he said.

"Why did you say nobody would want to settle down with you?"

Huh. Alice Bloom was a straight shooter.

He shifted on his feet, trying to decide how to answer. For some reason, he didn't think his usual bullshit was going to cut it here. The way he saw it, he could either divert her on to another subject, something safer. Like whether he took regular or decaf. Or, he could tell her the truth. Shut this down, before it really got started. Sure, the bet thing was fun. And, yeah. He'd really like to see her naked. But did he really have any intention of going beyond this? Beyond today, and this strange introduction to a world he'd never wanted to know anything about?

She looked melancholy, like she expected something of him, something he'd come to expect of himself a long time ago. She had to know he wasn't a good bet for someone like her. But attraction was a funny animal, and there was enough of it between them to cause a lot of trouble. A lot of trouble, indeed.

Instead of answering, instead of telling her the truth, or telling her he'd rather have that cup of coffee now, he stepped forward. He forced every single thought from his brain, and only kept room there for her. A spot that she'd occupied since the other night. Since he'd stared at that top button on her blouse, and began to fixate on it in a way that wasn't safe at all.

She watched him, tilting her head back as he approached. His heart thumped a steady rhythm in his chest. *Stop, stop, stop,* it seemed to say… Because he knew he'd just end up hurting her eventually. He always did.

Still, she looked so pretty standing there with her dark hair wild around her face, that he didn't want to stop. He wanted to forget his stupid conscience, and push her up against that vintage wallpaper. And what would she do if he did? The thought of her shoving him away registered briefly. But then the thought of her running her fingers through his hair took its place.

He kept his hands in his pockets. More out of necessity than anything else. If they were in his pockets, they couldn't be reaching for her hips.

"I'm going to be honest with you, Alice," he said, his voice low. "I'm not the settling-down type."

She nodded slowly. "Too boring?"

"I'm not saying it's not great for other people. I'm just a little…unconventional."

"And you don't want a girlfriend or wife telling you not to ride bulls…"

"That might have something to do with it."

He took another step closer, his boots thudding on the hardwood floor. There was a sound coming from the back of the house, but he barely noticed. Probably the ghost of some poor soul who didn't know they were dead yet. But at the moment, all Jake cared about was the way Alice's pulse was tapping at the hollow of her throat.

"Even though it'd be because they love you…" Her voice was hoarse. She looked nervous. Maybe because she could read his filthy mind.

"Sometimes love isn't enough," he said. "Have you ever heard that saying…caged birds don't sing?"

"I don't know about caged birds, but dead birds sure don't have anything to say."

He smiled at that. He was only a few inches away now. She wore a little makeup, but not much. The women he usually dated made an art form of their makeup—painting the stuff on like Rembrandt rodeo queens. It was really pretty impressive. But Alice wore so little, that he could see a scattering of freckles across her nose that he'd missed the other night. Her eyelashes were still dark and spiked from the rain, and he guessed this was probably how she looked right out of the shower. Not an unpleasant thought.

"I told you," he said. "I don't want to die."

"And I don't want you to die, either."

"Finally, something we agree on."

They watched each other, the electric currents sparking between them, growing stronger and harder to ignore. Jake figured if he got shocked enough, at some point he'd have to blink. The question was, when.

On the other side of the house, a door slammed. Somebody dropped their keys on a countertop, whistling a nameless tune.

Jake stepped back, and Alice smoothed her shirt as if he'd just had his hand up it.

"Alice?" a male voice called. "You home?"

"In here, Dad!" she called back. Then looked up at him apologetically. "It's my dad."

He smiled. "I figured."

"Don't worry. I won't introduce you as my boyfriend."

She was giving him a hard time. But if he'd been wearing a shirt with a collar, he'd want to loosen it. It had been a long time since he'd met anyone's dad. And for some reason, he didn't want Alice's father to assume he was some rough-around-the-edges stranger who'd just taken his only daughter for a ride on the back of his Harley. Which, he had.

"Hey, hon. I was just—"

Her dad walked in, stopping mid-sentence when he saw Jake standing there. Either Alice didn't get many visitors, or the visitors she did get didn't look like him. All of a sudden, he was aware of his old boots. His T-shirt, which still clung damply to his chest.

"Hi, there."

"Dad, this is Jake Elliott. Jake, this is my dad, Charles."

Jake stepped forward and extended his hand. The older man took it with a smile on his deeply lined face.

"Sir," Jake said. "Nice to meet you."

"Nice to meet you, son."

"Jake was a guest at Mrs. Chapman's service the other day," Alice added quickly. As if she wanted her dad to know there was a good reason Jake was back at the funeral home now. Like it was perfectly normal to pay your respects after paying your respects.

Charles Bloom rubbed his clean-shaven chin thoughtfully. He looked like someone Jake's grandpa would golf with. He wore a navy blue polo tucked neatly into khaki slacks, and a well-loved watch on his wrist. Jake liked him already.

"Elliott, Elliott," the older man said. "Why does that name sound familiar?"

"My family owns a farm here in Marietta."

"No, that's not it. Jake Elliott…" Charles snapped his fingers. "The PBR champ! Am I right?"

"Yes, sir."

"I can't say I've been to the rodeo recently, but I've heard how good you are. An injury has you sidelined for a bit, if I remember correctly? I think I read that in the *Courier*."

"That's right. A bum shoulder. But hoping to be back at it by the Copper Mountain Rodeo."

Alice watched this exchange like a tennis match, her gaze shifting from her dad, to Jake, then back again. "I never knew you followed rodeo, Dad," she said.

"Well, I don't. Not really, but this boy's a local star, honey." Charles looked them up and down. "Did you two get caught in the rain?"

"It's kind of a long story," she said. "Jake was nice enough to give me a ride home. My tire's flat."

"But you're all wet…"

"He rides a motorcycle."

The older man's bushy white brows rose. This obviously wasn't something he expected from his daughter. All of a sudden, Jake felt the ridiculous need to tell him that she'd worn a helmet, and he'd driven really slow.

"I was just about to grab some coffee to warm us up," she said. "You want to join us?"

"I'd like that. I just came over to fix that leaky faucet, but coffee sounds better." He turned to Jake. "Unless you two would rather be alone?"

Oh, God. Did it look like he wanted to be alone with Alice? Probably. What the hell was he doing here again?

"No, no, Dad." Alice reached out and touched her father's arm. Then looked over at Jake, horrified. "It's not like that. It's just coffee."

He was an asshole. Truly. He hoped her dad hadn't noticed the panicked look in his eyes just then. If he ever had a daughter, he'd sure as hell want better for her than a bull rider like him. He really didn't know why Alice scared him so much. Only that she made him feel exposed, and exposed people were opening themselves up to weakness. And Jake made a living out of proving to everyone in his life that he wasn't weak. Without meaning to, he pictured his little brother in that hospital bed all those years ago. Weak, sick. Lucky had almost died that summer.

Schooling his features, Jake smiled at the older man. "No, that sounds great."

Alice watched him, her face flushed. "Are you sure you don't have anywhere to be?"

"Nope. I'm good."

Apparently satisfied, she headed for the kitchen. "Be right back!" she called over her shoulder.

"Why don't we go in here," Charles said, motioning to the small room a few feet away. "The light's so nice this time of day."

Jake followed him inside where four red velvet upholstered chairs sat waiting. There was a dark mahogany desk by the window, with what looked like JCPenney catalogs open on top of it. Only these were for coffins, not back-to-school clothes. There were color swatches lurking off to the side. He didn't want to know what those were for.

But overall, the room was delicate, pretty. Making him feel, like the rest of the house, like he'd stepped back in time.

"Please," Charles said. "Sit."

Jake sat with a sigh, and rubbed his hands down his thighs. The chair was surprisingly comfortable. Jake noticed things like comfortable chairs these days. A side effect of getting beat to a pulp on a weekly basis.

Charles sat, too, crossing his legs and leaning forward like he might be getting ready to discuss burial arrangements.

"I'm sorry if I seemed surprised to see you here," the older man said, his voice low enough that Jake could tell he didn't want Alice to hear, even though she was all the way across the house. "I'm not used to her having people over on the weekends. I come and go pretty freely, but maybe I should stop doing that so much."

Jake didn't know what to say to that. The dynamic of living in a funeral home was strange enough. But it was a good insight into what a quiet life Alice must have. She seemed happy with her job, and she was good at it. Still, he wondered if she was lonely. The thought made him feel oddly protective of her. Like he wanted to wrap her in his arms and shield her from anyone who could hurt her.

"How do you two know each other, if you don't mind me asking?" Charles said.

"We don't really. Know each other. We met the other day at Elaine's service, and then ran into each other…" Should he mention the Wolf Den? She was a grown woman, but Charles Bloom didn't seem like the Wolf Den type. "Downtown," he finished lamely.

Charles nodded like he wasn't really buying all that, but at the same time, looking fine with it. Honestly, he just seemed happy to be having a chat. Jake, on the other hand, felt like a bull in a china shop sitting there next to him. He wondered if Alice had ever brought home a cowboy before. Somehow, he doubted it.

"Then I saw her this morning having some car trouble, and here we are."

"Thank you for that," Charles said. "I taught her how to change a tire when she started driving, but I guess it's been a while."

Jake wouldn't mention that she didn't have a spare. It was none of his business.

Parting the sheer curtains, Charles looked outside. The sun was starting to come out. It filled the room with warm, yellow light that spilled across the old, hardwood floor like melted butter.

"I'm glad she let you give her a ride," Charles said. "Alice is fiercely independent. But then, she's had to learn to be."

Jake frowned, watching him.

"Growing up in this place, the way she did…" Charles let the curtains swish back together. "Well, without her mother, and without very many close friends to lean on…she's had to nurture a strength she didn't know she had."

"She mentioned it was hard. That kids weren't so nice."

Charles smiled and studied his hands in his lap. "That's an understatement. Of course, she wouldn't go into details. And she wouldn't want me going on about it, either. It was a long time ago. But she had it fairly rough." Charles looked back up at Jake, and there was a sharpness behind his blue eyes that hadn't been there before. Jake had seen that same look in his own father's eyes too many times to count. It was the look of a parent who'd kick someone's ass from here until Sunday if they needed to.

"That's all I'll say about that," the older man continued. "But she deserves to be happy. Do you understand what I'm saying?"

Jake grit his teeth. It was impossible to know exactly what Charles thought his intentions were toward Alice, but this was a clear warning. The man obviously thought the sun rose and set on his daughter, and rightly so.

Jake realized then, that the responsible thing, the *right* thing to do, would be to stop this now. Before he and Alice got in over their heads. Before he had to break it off and contribute to what sounded like a long string of disappointments she'd had her whole life.

He nodded at the older man with the neatly combed hair, and the kind, no-nonsense expression on his face. "I understand, sir."

Charles smiled. "Good, good. Now tell me about this rodeo business. I used to have a horse named Penelope when I was a kid. I fell off once, broke my pinkie finger. It still aches when it snows, if you can believe that…"

Jake smiled back, listening politely. But he was still thinking about Alice. About how he'd just made the decision to steer clear, and how that absolutely was the right thing. But how it was also leaving him with a funny feeling inside his chest.

Maybe like that once-broken pinkie finger in the cold.

Chapter Six

ALICE HEADED DOWN the stairs of the basement, hearing Dana's music playing at a low level. It was Led Zeppelin, Dana's favorite band, and would've absolutely rattled the walls if cranked up on something other than their old transistor radio.

As far as Alice was concerned, the basement was where the hardest part of the funeral home business took place. The part that was scientific and detached. Dana didn't agree. She thought ushering the families through their grief was the hardest part. But in the end, the three people that made up Bloom Funeral Home all really complemented each other—using their own personal strengths, and working together to conquer each day the best way they knew how. They were a team now. And that felt good.

Still, Alice knew something had been bothering Dana this last week. She'd been quiet and withdrawn, and unwilling to talk much, if at all. To make things worse, Alice had been in her own funk, distracted by one Jake Elliott. Or more specifically, Jake Elliott's perfectly heartbreaking disappearing act. Since their coffee date that hadn't really been a date at all, he'd ghosted her in the most ghosty way possible. He now seemed to be nothing but a sexy memory in Wranglers.

Fighting an ache in her throat at the thought of him and those stupid jeans, she came the rest of the way down the stairs to see Dana working in the corner.

She stood over a gurney wearing a pink apron with little hearts all over it. She looked like she should be baking cookies instead of putting makeup on a corpse. But the apron humanized the job, and Alice loved her for it. It was a small way to bring some tenderness into a basement that didn't see a whole lot of tenderness at all.

Dana looked up and smiled. "What are you doing down here?"

"I just came to say hi. See how you were doing. How's Mr. Lopez?"

Dana glanced down at the elderly man on the gurney and smoothed his wispy hair. For being dead, he looked pretty happy. Like he'd finally gotten that nap he'd been waiting for. Like Mrs. Chapman, he'd also passed in his sleep after a long, fulfilling life. Alice wished they all could be like Mr. Lopez. Napping with a knowing smile and slightly disheveled hair.

"He's fine," Dana said. "We should be ready by one."

"The flowers just came. Dad's setting up. It'll be a full house. Apparently, he volunteered for Meals on Wheels, and ran a program matching shelter animals up with kids learning to read. Is there anything cuter than a first grader reading to a pit bull?"

Dana clutched her chest. "Are you serious?"

"Very."

The younger woman gazed down at Mr. Lopez and smiled. But she looked wistful, far away. And then, there was the unmistakable tremble of her bottom lip.

Alice stepped forward, not wanting to pry, but not being able to help it, either. "Dana…"

After a few seconds, her friend looked up. Her eyes were bright.

"What's going on?" Alice asked.

"Nothing."

"Dana…"

Wiping her eyes with the back of her fist, she frowned. "Nothing. It's just that he was such a good person. Probably a good dad. Sometimes I forget what those look like."

"Want to tell me about it?"

"There's nothing to tell. Really. I'm not going back."

Alice gazed at her friend. She was so street-smart and savvy that it was easy to forgot how young Dana really was. Right then, she looked like a little girl. And if the black eyeliner and piercings were designed to make people think she was tough, at the moment, they were failing miserably. Alice could see right through them.

"Back where?" she asked.

"Wisconsin."

"That's where your family lives?"

Dana nodded. Her eyes had filled with tears. Honest-to-goodness ones, that teetered on the edge of her thick, charcoal-colored lashes. They glistened briefly, then spilled onto her cheeks, making tracks down her pale skin.

"Oh, honey." Alice came around the gurney and put an arm around her. She was so petite, she felt like a delicate bird tucked into her side. "What happened?"

"My dad was just diagnosed with dementia. Can you believe that? At fifty-eight?"

"Oh no."

"My mom wants me to come home. Before it gets worse. I haven't been home in three years. He doesn't care about me. He doesn't care if I stay or go, he never has."

Her shoulders were shaking now, and she was having trouble keeping her voice even.

"I'm sure that's not true," Alice said. "He's your dad. Of course he cares."

"He doesn't. He doesn't agree with the way I live. He's ashamed of me."

"Dana, no."

"He is."

She was hiccupping now, crying in great, gulping sobs that were ripping Alice's heart in two. She knew the pain of losing her mother. She knew the heartache of never fitting in. But never in her life had she experienced the trauma of a parent turning her away. As wonderful as Dana was, it was hard to imagine. But at the same time, she wasn't so naïve in thinking this kind of thing didn't happen all the time.

Turning to her friend, Alice took her face in her hands. "I've heard you talk about your dad. I know you love him. And he loves you. Life is so short, Dana. So, so short. He probably wants to fix things between the two of you. Be even if he falls short, you'll know you tried, right?"

Dana sniffed, scowling at the wall behind Alice. "I can't go back. I won't."

Sighing, Alice dropped her hands to her sides. "I haven't walked in your shoes, so I can't say how I'd feel. But for me..." She paused, letting the moment stretch between them. "I'd give anything to have one more talk with my mom," she finally said. "To tell her how I feel."

Dana reached over poor Mr. Lopez who was oblivious that the conversation had taken a turn, and grabbed a Kleenex to wipe her nose. "But you and your mom were different. My dad has never accepted me. Ever. I just don't think I can do it. It's too..."

She didn't finish. And there was no telling what she was going to say, but for some reason, all Alice could think of was the word *scary*. That was something she understood. She understood letting fear dictate what she did and didn't do. To her very bones.

"You don't have to explain," she said. "I just want you to know I'm here if you ever need to talk. You've been so quiet this week. I was beginning to worry."

Dana wiped her nose, balled the tissue up, and threw it toward the trash can. She missed. They stood there, listening to the music coming from the little radio, letting it settle between them. It was comforting somehow, familiar—softening the sharpness of the conversation in a way that only music could.

After a long moment, Alice gave her friend a small smile, and turned to head back upstairs. She probably wanted to be alone for a while anyway. But Dana reached out and stopped her before she could.

"I'm not the only one who's been quiet," Dana said softly.

She turned back around. "Me?"

"Yeah, you."

"I've just been busy."

"Uh-huh."

"I have." Alice ran her hands down the front of her black slacks. "With work."

"No, you've been busy thinking about Jake. That's what you've been busy with."

"I haven't...not really."

Dana sighed, squeezing Alice's arm. "Does he have your number?

"I gave it to him. He'd call if he wanted to."

"Well, maybe he just needs a little push."

A little push... She was too proud to give him a little push. But deep down, there was another reason, a bigger reason why she didn't want to push. And by the way Dana was looking at her now, she thought her friend probably knew exactly what that was.

"Come on, Alice," Dana said. "You know you want to."

"It's just..."

"Just what?"

Alice trailed a finger over the edge of the cold, steel gurney. She could hear her dad upstairs. He was moving furniture around, setting the flowers out, fussing. The house felt especially peaceful today. But her heart ached anyway. She didn't even know Jake Elliott. Not well at least. But as each day went by without hearing from him, she was being forced to admit that he'd done something to her that first night—lit something inside her that she was having trouble putting out.

Looking over at her friend, she swallowed hard. Her tongue felt thick and dry in her mouth. "He kind of terrifies me," she said.

Dana watched her, quiet. Looking like a kindred spirit. Someone who was a polar opposite, but who understood completely.

"I don't know how to feel what I feel when I'm with him," she continued. "I'm afraid of what I'll do. I'm afraid to let go."

"I get it," Dana said. "I get being afraid."

Alice smiled. "You're not afraid of anything."

"You know that's not true. I'm afraid of going home. Of opening myself up to pain, same as you. But what's life without pain? Hurting a little means you're living, right?"

"I don't want to hurt."

Dana considered this, chewing her bottom lip where a small, silver ring caught the light. "You're just assuming he'll hurt you. But what if he doesn't?"

Alice laughed. "You've seen the guy. What are the odds?"

"Fifty-fifty. But maybe you're the heartbreaker in this scenario."

"Ha."

"I'd love to see the look on his face if you tracked him down. For real this time. No driving around town where you think you might catch a lame-o glimpse."

Alice's face burned.

"You could do it, you know," Dana continued. "We know where he hangs out on Saturday nights. Just say screw it, and take the bull by the horns. See what happens."

Shaking her head, Alice stepped away from the gurney. She wasn't that brave. "I have to get back upstairs."

"Alice."

Stopping, she looked back at her friend.

"Don't be like me," Dana said evenly. Her eyes were still red, puffy. The pain from a few minutes ago still etched on her face.

"What do you mean?"

"I mean, don't be a chickenshit, Alice."

Chapter Seven

Alice sat with her car idling in the dark parking lot, the windows rolled down to let the soft, evening breeze caress her bare shoulders.

With trembling hands, she reached up to adjust the rear-view mirror, and gazed at her reflection. She wore more makeup than usual tonight. She'd been worried she wouldn't get it right, but had to admit the smoky eye shadow made her eyes pop. Overall, she looked like a woman in her mid-thirties going out for a night on the town. Nobody had to know she didn't usually go out for nights on the town. Or that her pushup bra was poking her in the under-boob.

Taking a breath, she reached over and grabbed her purse. There'd been so many things that had brought her to this moment—the lighthearted bet with Jake, for one. The not-so-lighthearted advice from Dana, for another. The memories from her childhood, the pain of losing her mother, the fear of losing anyone else, had all settled in her mind and worked their way into her heart, until she'd simply wanted to scream at the world. She was sick and tired of being afraid.

Going out to find Jake might be a mistake. But to her, it was one worth making. She had to know if she'd ever see him browsing through a bookstore, or walking in a park just to breathe in the scent of fresh flowers. She wanted to see him discovering the things she loved, even if it meant stepping outside her comfort zone to do it. Even if it meant he might not want the same. It was a very real possibility.

But that's where she'd forced herself to stop thinking. It was impossible to be brave if she kept going over and over the ways she could fail. For the first time in her life, Alice had shoved those thoughts aside, and shaved her legs like a champ. Who knew how tonight would turn out? He might not even be there, but the excitement of not knowing was part of the ride.

With her heart pounding in her chest, she opened the car door and stepped out into the velvety night air. Raucous voices from the Wolf Den carried across the parking lot, and she could smell the cigarette smoke from outside the doors. She'd always hated the smell of tobacco, but now it reminded her of the night she met Jake, so her brain didn't really know what to do with that. Her stomach tightened as she thought of him sitting there on that barstool. Broad shoulders; thick, silky hair. The wide, sexy smile that was confident enough for the both of them.

Smoothing the emerald green dress she'd only worn once before, she looked down, and wondered if he'd like it. It was form-fitting with a wide, black, patent leather belt. The neckline dipped, but didn't plunge, and she wore her favorite black, strappy heels that complemented her new pedicure. It might be too much. But what if it was? At the very least, she'd conquered this particular fear, and her toes would be sandal-worthy for a month.

She put her purse over her shoulder and made her way toward the bar's entrance, making sure not to twist her ankle in any of the potholes in the parking lot. A couple of cowboys walked past and looked her up and down. She glanced back nervously, wondering if that was a good sign.

Chewing the inside of her cheek, she walked through the door that was propped open with an empty barstool. Country music thumped in her ears, mixed with the sound of laughter and talking, and pool balls smacking together. Someone walked by carrying a plate of beer-battered onion rings, and the smell made Alice's stomach growl. She'd held off on dinner in order to get the dress zipped past her hips. Now, she wished she'd eaten, and worn a pair of jeans instead.

She rubbed her damp palms down her thighs and looked around. The place was hopping, just like on her birthday. People were crowded near the bar, and almost every table was full. Only tonight, she wasn't here with Dana. Didn't have the comfort of seeing her friend playing pool from across the room, or knowing they'd be having a quick drink and leaving soon. Tonight, she was very much alone. Suddenly, she was clammy, hot. Feeling like a throbbing big toe sticking out of a shoe three sizes too small.

And Jake was nowhere in sight.

The strange confidence that had overtaken her earlier began to vanish. What in the world was she doing here? Even the incredibly powerful temptation of seeing Jake again, wasn't enough of an explanation.

Some people at the bar had turned to look at her. She felt like she was in junior high again, the target of everyone's morbid curiosity.

Smiling at them, she took a step backward. Maybe this was the beginning of some kind of midlife crisis. She'd skipped the sports car, and gone straight for the Spanx and younger cowboy. Her face burned. So much for fearlessness.

She took another step back, and bumped into someone, nearly grinding her heel into their boot.

"I'm sorry," she mumbled. "I—"

But before she could finish, she felt warm breath on the side of her neck. It sent chills all the way up into her hair.

"Well, if it isn't Marietta's hottest funeral home director."

Alice's stomach dropped to her knees. The voice was low and thick. It was loud in the bar, but she'd know it anywhere.

Closing her eyes for a brief second, she gathered her courage. *Fearless, fearless, fearless...*

She opened them again, and turned around. Jake stood there gazing down at her, the expression on his handsome face pinning her in place. The cockiness she'd remembered was there—the slight tilt to his mouth, the teasing looking in his eyes. But there was an unmistakable hunger, too. She knew, because she'd seen it in her own eyes when she'd gotten ready earlier. Looking into the mirror and thinking about what it would be like to fall into his arms. She'd imagined every scenario possible, and still, the steamy daydream didn't compare to the smoking reality of him standing within reach now.

Jake held a bottle of beer by the neck, lifting it to his mouth to take a pull. He never took his eyes off her. He swallowed, his Adam's apple bobbing up and down. The moment seemed to last forever, and that was just fine by her.

"What are you doing here, Alice Bloom?" he asked.

Alice gazed up at him. *What am I doing here?* A minute ago she couldn't remember. But now, as that familiar electric current pulsed between them, it all came rushing back.

She balled her hands into fists at her sides, and then forced them to relax again. "I was hoping to see you," she said.

He let his honeyed gaze slip down her body. "In that dress? Are you trying to kill me?"

A distinctive heat crept over her chest. Never in her life had a man's words affected her like this. He hadn't even touched her, and she was already shaking from the inside out.

She didn't answer. She had no idea what to say. But as luck would have it, she didn't have to say anything at all. He reached out and took her hand in his. It was big and cal-loused, swallowing hers whole. Every single nerve ending in her fingers, her palm, her wrist, sparked and caught fire.

"Dammit," he said. "I was trying to keep my distance. You had to know that."

"I figured."

"But you came here anyway."

She shrugged, going for blasé, and somehow pulling it off.

"This doesn't seem like your style," he said.

"It's not."

"It took guts."

"Dana told me I shouldn't be a chickenshit."

He smiled, pulling her closer. "I like Dana."

He smelled like soap and deodorant. This close, she could see his strawberry blond eyelashes were longer than she'd thought. He wasn't wearing his hat tonight, but the distinctive ring around his hair remained, something that made her ovaries twitch.

There was a sudden stab of fear in her wary heart. She could actually *feel* herself falling for him. Helplessly out of control. And just what would she do when the ground came rushing at her without a net?

The music coming from the jukebox died down, and then something slow by Keith Urban came crooning forth.

"Dance with me?" he asked, squeezing her hand.

"I don't think...I don't think there's dancing?"

"Sure there is." He leaned over and set his beer on the table next to them. "Come on."

Pulse fluttering, she let him lead her through the crowd. There was a spot by the pool table that was relatively clear of people. He guided her right to the middle of it, and turned to face her.

Not waiting for him to step close, she went on her own. This time, there was no thinking, no weighing the cost. There was only the need to satisfy an intense female craving that had taken her completely off guard.

He wrapped a muscled arm around her waist, the hard

ridges of his belt buckle pushing into her hip. He gazed down at her, and began moving slowly to the music. She followed his lead. Honestly, at that point, she would've followed him anywhere. All the other people in the stuffy, packed bar seemed to fall away then. It was just the two of them, dancing, in the moment, reveling in the undeniable heat between them.

She stared up at him. "So, you were trying to stay away from me, huh?"

He nodded.

"Is that why you didn't call?" she asked. "Not because you didn't want to?"

Laughing a little at that, he moved his thumb in a lazy half-arc over her lower back. "Darlin, I wanted to. And that's exactly why I didn't."

"Because you're not the settling-down type."

"Because I don't want to hurt you."

He was being honest, and a part of her loved that. But there was a small part, an irrational part, that wished he'd just lie to her. Just for tonight. Let her think the same wildness that she loved about him could be tamed so she could love him.

"I know you don't," she said.

"We both know where this could go. And someone like you deserves more."

Her heart beat steadily inside her chest. Painfully. "Well, I'm not looking to get married," she said, forcing a smile. "And to tell you the truth, you scare me too much, anyway. I know me, and I know I couldn't let myself get close to you if

I was only going to get crazy every time you walked into an arena."

"So, we're a match made in hell."

"I wouldn't say in hell, but I know you're not going to ask me to go steady, and I wouldn't trust you if you did."

He slid his hand up her back, and the slow and steady movement nearly made her knees buckle. "So, now what?" he asked, watching her reaction. Probably liking that he had that kind of power over her.

"We keep it casual. Be friends, have some fun. Maybe take that bet once and for all."

He smiled, leaning close. She could feel his breath, warm against her face. *Oh, God.* How could she ever keep something like this casual? Not letting him break her heart was going to take every ounce of strength she had. But it was either that, or walk away. And that kind of strength, she just didn't have.

"Can I ask you a question," he said, brushing his lips against her ear. "Friend to friend?"

Chills sprouted along her arms. He was making her entire body hum, and she had a feeling he wasn't even trying.

"Of course."

"Did you wear this for me?"

She felt his hand splayed across her spine, its heat through her dress. She liked the subtle possessiveness of it. She was in way over her head, and she knew that. But she wasn't that interested in coming up for air, either.

"Maybe," she managed. "Do you like it?"

"I like it. But I'd be lying if I said I didn't like that blouse from the other night better."

She felt her eyes widen. "From my birthday?"

That blouse had been in her wardrobe for the last five years, at least. It had seen church services, holidays, ordinary workdays. It was one of her favorites, but only because it was silk, something that felt kind of exotic on an ordinary workday. But it wasn't exactly sexy.

"Why?" she asked.

"That top button?" He touched the hollow of her throat with his index finger. "Just begging to be undone? Come on."

"Huh."

"But this dress…" Keith was still killing it from the jukebox, and another couple had begun dancing nearby. They were starting a trend. "This dress does *not* scream funeral home director, Alice Bloom."

"What does it scream?"

"It screams wild woman. Hot dress today, skinny-dipping tomorrow."

She laughed. "Right."

"Seriously, though. You know what this means…"

"What?"

"Now it's my turn. You had the balls to come here to-night. Which means you're one up on me. Which means—"

"Bookstore time," she interrupted, grinning.

Keith's velvety voice died away from the jukebox, and the room grew momentarily quiet. Jake let his hands drop to her hips as they stood there staring at each other. For one panty-dropping second, she thought he was going to lean down and kiss her. She wanted him to. She was aching for it. But at the same time, she understood that keeping it casual didn't necessarily mean giving in to that particular urge. That when and if they took that step, both of them were going to have a hard time reining it in, and hadn't he just said he didn't want to hurt her?

No, it was much better to keep him at arm's length. To flirt, have some fun, to live a little. To a reasonable extent, of course. She'd learn from him, and he'd learn from her. They'd be friends, like she'd said. And when it was all said and done, maybe she'd even go see him ride at the Copper Mountain Rodeo in the fall. Maybe by then it wouldn't bother her so much. Maybe.

Instead of kissing him like she really wanted to, and like her dress absolutely said she'd been planning to, she reached out to shake his hand.

He smiled down at her, curiously.

"I have a great bookstore I'd like to show you," she said. "Let's shake on it."

Chapter Eight

J AKE LEANED AGAINST the old stall door, the sun filtering
in through the slats in the barn roof, warming the back of
his neck. It was already hot, would probably be close to
ninety by mid-afternoon, and it didn't look like much of the
fence work he'd come out to Sleigh Bell for today was going
to get done.

"She's getting close," Lucky said, turning his White Sox
cap around backwards, and wiping a trickle of sweat from his
face. "Shouldn't be long now."

Jake watched Lucky's paint mare, Pop Tart, pace her
heavily bedded stall. Fat veins stood out on her swollen belly,
and her silky black tail kept swishing busily at flies. He had
no idea what it was like to have a baby, but Jake felt for her.
She looked like she was about to pop.

"That's it, mama," his cousin Jenny murmured to his
right. "It's okay."

On Jake's left, Jesse leaned on the stall door too, his
cowboy hat pushed up off his forehead. "Is it terrible to say
this is great timing? I didn't want to check fences today."

Jenny smirked. "Hung over, Jess?"

"No. Just lazy."

Lucky stacked some clean towels outside the stall. Jake liked watching his little brother work like this. Lucky was happiest taking care of animals. He'd almost become a vet like their dad, but had converted part of the sprawling family farm into an animal sanctuary instead—a long-held dream. He ran the place with the precision of a drill sergeant, but with the heart of an absolute giant.

Jake rubbed the back of his neck, breathing in the sweet smell of hay and horse. Deep down, he'd always wanted to be more like his little brother. Able to shed those terrible weeks and months after the fire that had almost taken Lucky's life, and grow from the experience. But Jake seemed to have stopped growing the second they'd airlifted his ten-year-old brother to Billings that day. As the helicopter took flight, so had Jake's sense of being grounded in any relationship that really mattered. He'd lived the next sixteen years pushing away any feeling of vulnerability or tenderness. He understood this about himself, and he recognized the irony of lecturing Alice about her fear, when it was fear with all its sharp teeth that had cornered him into living only for himself as an adult.

Lowering her head, Pop Tart nudged the straw with her pink nose, then turned in a full circle as if getting ready to lie down. But then changed her mind with a heavy sigh.

"God, she looks uncomfortable," Jenny said.

Jesse shook his head. "No doubt. And little does she know, life as she knows it is about to be *over*."

Jenny shot him a look. "What's that supposed to mean?"

"Motherhood. You know."

"No, I don't know."

One of Jesse's favorite pastimes was needling his cousin. And she was always game to needle right back. It should've been an Olympic sport.

Lucky gave them some side-eye, before going back to watching his mare.

"Having kids ties you down, Jen," Jesse went on. "Once you settle in with a family..." He made a clicking sound. "It's the end of the line as far as excitement goes."

"Good Lord," Jenny said. "You're a Neanderthal."

Jesse shrugged, not bothering to argue. "Ask Jake," he said. "He'll tell you."

"Don't drag me into this."

"I'm not asking Jake," Jenny said, "because Jake is the *worst* example of anyone wanting a family of anyone I know. No offense, Jake."

"None taken."

"By the way," she continued. "I ran into Becky the other day..."

He raised his brows, careful not to bite. Jenny loved bringing up his ex-girlfriend, because it fit her narrative of how he kept letting happiness slip right through his fingers. And yeah, he'd let her go. But they hadn't been right for each other anyway.

Still, he didn't like to talk about it. Not because he still loved her, but because there was a tiny, nagging part of himself that wondered if Jenny had a point. Most of the time he told himself he liked being alone. But sometimes, when the evening sky was a certain shade of pastel, or his bed felt just a little too chilly in the middle of winter, he thought about what it would be like to share his life with someone. But then he shut the thought out as fast as it tried to worm its way in. He didn't need to share his life with someone in order for it to be full. He had his career. He had enough adventure to shake a stick at, which was all he'd ever wanted.

Not waiting for an answer, Jenny turned to him, her copper-colored hair falling over one eye. "She said to tell you hi," she said, tucking it behind one ear again. "Asked how the riding is going."

He nodded, biting his tongue. He didn't need to add fuel to this particular fire.

"That baby sure is cute," she continued. "That could've been your baby, you know."

"Oh, Jesus, Jenny." This time he couldn't help it. "Stop trying to marry me off. Has it ever occurred to you I might like my life the way it is?"

"Lonely?"

"Who says I'm lonely?"

"You didn't look so lonely the other night." This from Jesse who was eyeing him like a seventh grader.

"What?"

"I mean, if that dark-haired lady you were dancing with at the Wolf Den was any indication."

Jenny perked up at this brand new information. Even Lucky looked over as Pop Tart finally lowered herself into the straw with a groan.

Jake's neck heated. He hadn't exactly been trying to hide how Alice affected him in that dress.

"Oh?" Jenny said. "Who's this?"

"Nobody."

"The funeral home director from over at Bloom's," Jesse offered up. "I asked around."

Jenny's mouth hung open. "Oh, no you didn't."

"Did *what*? I just danced with her."

"Don't you dare go breaking her heart, Jake, or I'll come after you myself."

"I'm not planning on breaking anyone's heart." He was trying not to. He really was. "And how do you know her?"

"I don't. I know *of* her, and she seems like a really nice person, who probably has no idea what she's getting herself into."

"Thanks?"

Pop Tart lay on her side, her round belly jutting into the air. Her breathing came faster as a contraction washed over her. Her long legs stiffened, and she groaned softly.

Jake loosened his collar, feeling hot. "Aren't you going in there, Luck?"

"Not until the baby starts coming. I'll cut the sack if I need to, clear the nose, but right now I just want to give her some space."

Jenny nodded as if she understood completely. Jake did too, recalling all those sitcoms where laboring moms chucked things at people's heads when they walked through the door. Pop Tart lacked the opposable thumbs to chuck anything, but her hooves would do a pretty good job on their own. Space was probably a good idea.

"I heard she was a little strange," Jesse said.

"Who?" Jake asked, still watching the horse.

"Alice Bloom."

He turned on his brother, suddenly irritated. "Who told you that?"

Jesse held up both hands. "Sorry, just what I heard."

"Probably from the same dumbasses who haven't evolved past the tenth grade. And just because she works in a funeral home, doesn't make her strange, dude."

"I was just—"

Jake loved his brother. But judging by the way he was feeling now, he might have to split Jesse's lip the next time Alice's name came out of his mouth. "Just don't," he said, his voice low and even. "Okay?"

Jenny, on the other hand, looked like she'd just struck gold. She smiled and crossed her arms over her chest. "I'm sensing you might actually like this one, Jake."

"Yeah, I like her. So what?"

"So, this is a nice change."

Was he that bad? He didn't ask, because he didn't want to know the answer. But his reaction just now had taken him off guard, too. The lightning-quick instinct to defend her.

Scowling, he focused on Pop Tart again, who was in the middle of another contraction. She groaned as two little hooves appeared below her tail.

Lucky opened the stall door and walked in to stand in the corner. The horse was laboring hard now, her breathing heavy and fast.

"You can do it, mama," Jenny said under her breath.

Suddenly, they were all on the same page as the quiet

energy in the barn turned to the sweet black and white mare who was trying so hard to bring a new life into the world. Jake didn't consider himself a softie by any stretch, but there was something about this that was getting to him. It was undeniable. There was a tightness in his throat that was making it hard to breathe.

Jenny's words from before nagged at him. He'd always been perfectly content living his life as the badass bachelor. There'd been some girlfriends, but they never really stuck around long. And could he blame them? What did he have to offer except being some kind of novelty—the bull rider who was a conversation starter at best? That had always been okay with him. Convenient, even. But what about when it wasn't okay anymore? What kind of life was he building for the long haul?

The question made him uncomfortable, because it was one he'd been ignoring for a very long time. And when those short-term girlfriends had brought it up, brought up how they were starting to have feelings for him, and wished he'd stop treating his life so recklessly, well then. That was when it was time to say sayonara, baby.

He grit his teeth, feeling his jaw muscles bunch almost painfully as he watched Pop Tart work through another contraction. The little hooves were now two long legs and a nose. Lucky knelt next to the horse and with expert precision, broke the sack around the foal and cleared its small nostrils. Then stood back again, giving mom and baby room.

"Oh my God," Jenny said. "It's a miracle, isn't it?"

She wasn't talking to anyone in particular. But Jake felt

the question go deep. For some reason, he thought of Becky right then, and her own rosy-cheeked baby. What would Jake's legacy be? A lifetime of Saturday nights at the Wolf Den, some broken bones, and an uncanny ability to stay unattached at any cost? For the very first time in his life, the brief thought seemed lonesome, sad. And that scared the shit out of him.

Suddenly, he pushed away from the stall door.

Jenny and his brothers looked over.

"I just remembered...I have somewhere I have to be," he mumbled.

"What?" Jenny said. "Now? You'll miss the foal."

Jake grabbed his Stetson from a nail on the wall and jammed it on his head. He had to get out of there, out of the stuffiness of the barn and the peculiar feeling that had settled itself on his chest.

"Text me a picture," he said.

And walked out the door.

Chapter Nine

ALICE WALKED DOWN the aisle slowly, trailing a finger along the dark wood bookshelves, lined with dog-eared paperbacks that smelled like heaven itself. She was in the mystery section, her favorite, but kept sneaking glances at Jake, who was in the self-help section.

She smiled, making sure she was hidden behind a large display of local chocolates. He looked huge standing there in his blue plaid shirt and Wranglers. Out of place in the slightly cramped space of the bookstore. He was rubbing the back of his neck and holding a book with a professional-looking woman on the cover. She had her arms crossed over her chest as if she knew the answer to something you didn't. Which, she probably did. *Unlocking the Secret to Your Success*—read the cover in big, no-nonsense lettering. *Discover What's Holding You Back in Today's Market.*

He frowned, and turned it over to squint at the back-cover blurb. A woman wearing a sweatshirt with the American flag embroidered on it squeezed by him, and he moved aside, mumbling an apology with a *ma'am* thrown in for good measure.

Alice's heart swelled. She couldn't tell yet if he was enjoying himself. The ride over to Bozeman had been relatively quiet. He'd suggested taking his Harley, and she'd refused, telling him it was possible to have a good time without being on a motorcycle. She was living proof. He'd grudgingly complied, and they'd stopped at a coffee shop on the way into town, getting two iced mochas to go, so they had something to drink in the bookstore.

She stood there now, bringing the coffee to her lips to take a sip. Watching Jake stuff the book back on the shelf, she tried to remember if she'd ever had any close guy friends before. There'd been a nerdy boy from her freshman-year geometry class who'd always let her borrow his ruler. They'd bonded over the latest season of *Friends*. And then there'd been Nick what's-his-face in college who used to sit with her in the cafeteria when there'd been a shortage of girlfriends around. There always seemed to be a shortage of girlfriends around. She remembered feeling awkward all the time, paranoid that she smelled like formaldehyde from biology class. Good times.

But other than those two, she really couldn't think of any time when she'd bonded with a guy before. Certainly, couldn't think of a time that she'd been this attracted to one, *then* embarked on a friendship of any kind. This whole thing had a Ross and Rachel vibe going on, and she wasn't sure yet if that was good or not. The only thing she knew for sure was that she wanted to savor every last minute of seeing him browse a few feet away. His big, rough hands thumbing through the yellowed pages of the used paperback, his hazel eyes holding a look of concentration, like he might be asked a book club question any second now.

Licking her lips and tasting the bittersweet mocha there, she started to head the other way, but stopped when she heard him walk up behind her.

"Hey," he said.

She turned and smiled. "Hey, yourself."

"It smells funny in here."

"It smells like books." She closed her eyes and breathed deeply. Then opened them again to see him watching her. "Now you try it," she said.

"Breathe?"

"Breathe in the scent. It reminds me of going to the library when I was a kid. Sometimes..." She paused, wondering if she should just shut it. They were there to introduce him to the things she loved, and he'd have a hard time liking them too, if all she did was babble on about her sad stories.

But the way he was looking down at her now gave her courage. She felt safe with him. She knew he wouldn't judge her for embarrassing things like not having very many friends growing up.

Gripping the shoulder strap on her purse, she went on. "Sometimes, I used to spend all afternoon at the library. The summer after my mom died, I'd show up first thing in the morning, and was usually the last one to leave. The librarian called me Apple, because I'd always carry one for lunch. Food wasn't allowed, but she always looked the other way." She smiled. "It was a place I could go to forget. It's hard to forget about death when you live in a funeral home."

Jake watched her for another minute, absorbing this. Then closed his eyes and took a deep breath. Her heart fluttered as she waited for him to open them again.

"Huh," he said. "My first impression is mothballs."

She shoved him in the arm.

"But I get it," he said.

"You do?"

"It's like the smell of manure."

"Manure."

"Not *fresh* manure, but yeah. It reminds me of the farm. Of my brothers and my grandparents. Of learning to ride horses. It brings it all back. It's weird how certain smells do that."

"It is. I hate the smell of Chanel Number Five. I had an aunt who wore it. She used to make me rub her feet."

"That'll do it."

They began walking down the aisle together, their arms brushing every now and then.

"I hate the smell of smoke," Jake said. "It makes me want to puke."

"Cigarette smoke?"

"No, smoke, smoke. From a fire."

"Why?"

He stopped and picked up a book. Something by Stephen King. They'd wandered into the horror section. Her second favorite.

"*The Shining* gave me nightmares for months," he mumbled. "I read it when I was ten. But nobody could tell me anything."

She watched as he put the book back on the shelf, but tenderly this time. Like it had some meaning.

"Why do you hate the smell of smoke?" she asked. Pressing him. Just a little.

Putting his hands in his pockets, he looked over her head, somewhere across the store. The muscles in his jaw bunched and relaxed. She got the feeling he was deciding whether or not to answer.

But then his gaze settled on her again, and his expression softened some.

"My brother set our barn on fire when we were kids," he finally said. "He almost died. I can't even have a fire in my woodstove. Makes me sick."

He shrugged, and it was obvious he didn't want to talk about it anymore, so she didn't respond. But she wanted to. She wanted to ask him about the fire, about what happened afterward, about his entire childhood. She wanted to open him up like one of the lovely books on the shelves surrounding them, and read his story from beginning to end. She didn't know Jake well, but she knew him well enough to realize he wasn't the kind of man you could push into talking. Either he did, or he didn't. She considered herself lucky he'd agreed to breathe in the smell of books and sip iced mocha with her. That was definitely progress. It was almost enough to make her think she had a shot at winning this crazy bet they had going on. Almost.

She reached out and spun a bookmark display, watching it slow, then stop like something on *The Price is Right!*

He walked up, then reached around her to pluck one off

the display. He was so close, she could feel the heat coming off his body. Her mouth went dry.

"Here's one for you," he said, holding it in front of her face.

It was an outline of a voluptuous woman reading a book. *Reading Is Sexy,* it said in hot pink bubble letters.

"Yeah, right," she said.

"You don't think reading is sexy, or you don't think *you're* sexy?"

All of a sudden, she felt their age difference yawn between them like the Grand Canyon. Was she sexy? Thirty-four wasn't exactly ancient, but he was probably used to much younger women. Twenty-two-year-olds whose thighs didn't jiggle in yoga class. Twenty-two-year-olds who actually *went* to yoga class. These days, Alice's idea of exercise was walking to the coffee pot in the mornings and back. She'd have to work on that.

"I think I'm okay," she said.

"Jesus. What an understatement."

Her face heated. Now they were getting into territory she wanted to steer clear of. She'd always had a skewed sense of her looks, outdated and politically incorrect. She had a tendency to tie them to her worth as a woman, even though she knew that was beyond antiquated. And she couldn't blame how she'd been raised either, as her dad had done all he could to build her self-esteem. But it still wavered. It was why going to the bar the other night in her practically new dress had been such a big deal. Alice didn't go to bars in dresses. Alice didn't go to bars period, because bars were where rejection occurred, and she'd had enough rejection to last a lifetime.

Jake tapped the bookmark to his lips, watching her.

"You don't know where that's been," she said evenly.

He held the bookmark out and looked at it. "This?"

She nodded.

"Uh, I'm guessing on the bookmark rack?"

"But people have probably picked it up, fingered it." She was embarrassing herself. But she couldn't help it.

"Oh, God. It's gonna be harder than I thought."

"What?"

"Getting you to loosen up, Alice."

"I'm plenty loose, Jake." It was hard to say that with a straight face, but she somehow managed it.

"Oh?"

"Yes."

"Where's the girl from the Wolf Den the other night, huh? That girl wouldn't be worried about bookmark germs."

"That's where you're wrong. She's always been afraid of bookmark germs, she was just hiding it well."

"Really, *really* well."

She shrugged.

"Which brings me to this…" he said, reaching around her to put the offending bookmark back. Little did future customers know that Jake Elliott's lips had touched it. Practically kissed it. Which made her a little weak in the knees. She was tempted to go buy the damn thing herself.

"Brings you to what?" she said.

His gaze settled on her again. "All those irrational fears of yours. We've got to start working on those. Exposure therapy. You know."

She did know. Her dad had taken her to a counselor once when she was a kid. She'd refused to go back, and he hadn't forced it.

"Let's just explore this for a minute, shall we?"

He wiggled a pair of imaginary glasses. It should've been annoying, but it wasn't. It was actually having the opposite effect.

She stopped herself before smiling at him.

"What are you afraid of right this minute?" he asked. "Not counting the bookmark. I put that back, so you're not in any immediate danger."

She rolled her eyes. "Where's the bathroom? I have to go."

She tried walking around him, but he held her arm.

"Wait just a minute there, little lady. We're about to make some progress here. What are you afraid of? Right now?"

The heat from his hand was burning into her upper arm, practically branding it. All she could picture was it on her bare skin, and her stomach tightened.

"Right now?"

He nodded.

"Wetting my pants in public."

"Okay. What else?"

"If I tell you, will you let me go?"

He took his hand off her arm, breaking her heart a little. "Sure. Go wherever you want, but I don't think you want to."

"Really."

"Really. I think you want to stay right here and work toward that skinny-dipping goal. One little fear at a time."

She laughed. "You're unbelievable."

"What else are you afraid of? And be honest this time."

"You." *Oh, God.* That had slipped out before she could help it.

"Me."

She refused to look him in the eyes. Focusing instead on the restroom sign across the bookstore. She didn't really have to go that bad, but she did want to escape.

"You're afraid of me," Jake repeated, his tone flat.

She nodded. This wasn't going to end well, since he was hell-bent on making her face her fears. And if he was one of those fears, just what kind of exposure therapy would he have up his sleeve? She could only guess.

"Well, this is interesting," he said.

"Not really. We've already been over this, remember? We're attracted to each other—"

"I don't know if we ever acknowledged it flat out, but I like where this is going."

"We're attracted to each other," she went on, ignoring him. "But we're going to stay friends and have these microbets, yada, yada, yada."

"Oh, right. I remember now. I'm a commitment-phobe, and you're afraid you're going to fall in love with me."

He'd just said love. Alice's ears burned.

"Something like that."

"What if I fall in love with you first? Hypothetically speaking."

Her tongue was suddenly so thick in her mouth, it felt like she was going to choke on it. She cleared her throat. "Doesn't matter. End result is the same. Commitment-phobe, remember?"

"Right. And there's also the part where you'd want me to quit rodeo, which is a hard pass. So that's a problem."

She squared her shoulders, and gazed up at him, this time narrowing her eyes a little.

"You don't have to keep reminding me that there's no give and take in your world, Jake. I get it."

"Ouch?"

"Yeah."

"I guess I deserved that. But you're not denying you'd want me to quit."

"I have no idea what I'd want, because I haven't been in that position." That was a lie. She didn't think she could love him, and watch him trying to kill himself at the same time. But he also had a point, as selfish as she thought it was. Asking him to change for her wouldn't be fair, either. She just believed love was a two-way street. There had to be some kind of compromise. Otherwise, he was going to be alone forever. But maybe that's what he wanted. Truly. And who was she to argue?

"Huh," he said, putting his hands in his pockets and rocking forward on his boots. "We're an interesting study, aren't we? It doesn't seem like there's a scenario where we'd ever work out, but we can't seem to stop spending time together, either."

"We're friends. That's what friends do."

"I usually sleep with all my female friends."

"*Jake.*"

"What about you? Many guy friends?"

As much as she wanted to count the kid in geometry, she couldn't, in good faith. "No," she said. "This is a first. I think it's going pretty well, though. Considering."

"Considering what?"

"That you keep harping on all my quirks and won't let the skinny-dipping thing die. But that's okay, because the opera thing isn't dying, either."

He groaned.

"I'm going to the bathroom now," she said.

"Wait. One more second. This'll be really quick."

She stared up at him.

"You got me into this bookstore, correct? I actually sniffed paperbacks today."

"True."

"Which means it's your turn now."

Her heart skipped a beat. What exactly did he have in mind? Judging by the look on his face, it wasn't necessarily safe. He wore that cocky smile, his eyes sparkling.

"My turn..." she repeated dumbly. She was having a hard time concentrating on the words that were coming out of his mouth. He was too good-looking. She'd never really thought that was a thing before. That someone could be *too* good-looking. But it was. Jake was too handsome for his own good.

Nodding, he stepped forward. Close. Really close. Close enough that other people in the bookstore might wonder what they were up to behind the bookmark display. She realized then, that along with Jake's good looks, came a social etiquette blocker of sorts. She really didn't care who saw what. She was only concerned with the thin, white scar on the side of his right eye. With his scruffy jaw. With his lips, and that smile that was doing inconvenient things to her insides.

"Your turn to step outside your comfort zone, Alice Bloom." He was whispering now, because, why not? It felt like they were standing in the middle of a bedroom. But there was no bed. Only a few threadbare chairs, and a teenage girl snapping her gum in the YA section.

She swallowed with some difficulty. "By doing what?"

"Kiss me," he said.

"What? No."

"Why not?"

"Oh, I don't know. Only a *gazillion* reasons."

"Name one."

"We're friends." Her voice sounded raspy and strained. Her poor vocal cords. She was surprised they were functioning at all.

"Bullshit."

"You said yourself you don't commit."

"I'm talking about one kiss. An experiment, so to speak. A micro-bet."

"That's a bad idea. A baaaaad idea."

He grinned slowly. "I'm all about bad ideas."

"Yeah, I know. That's what I'm afraid of."

He held his hands up. "I promise. One kiss. Push the boundaries. Get your heart pumping."

"You're assuming it'll pump."

He stared at her. It was already pumping. Right out of her chest. And he knew it.

She cleared her throat and let her gaze fall to his throat. To where the collar of his shirt gaped open just enough to show where his pulse tapped. His skin was bronzed and warm-looking. She wondered what he looked like shirtless. Like a God, probably. She pictured him working outside on his family farm, shirtless. Or getting ready to climb on the back of a bull, shirtless. Or vacuuming his living room floor…well, she was doing absolutely nothing to calm her nerves, here.

He hooked a finger underneath her chin and lifted it until she had no choice but to look him in the eyes again.

"Oh, I know it'll pump," he said. "That's the whole point."

Sometime in the last thirty seconds, her hands had started shaking. She crossed her arms over her chest, tucking them into her armpits to steady them. He was going to break her heart. Pulverize it, more likely. And she had nobody to blame but herself. She'd gone to the bar the other night all dressed up, and telling herself it had something to do with tackling her fears. When more to the point, she wasn't ready to let him say goodbye yet.

Well, he wasn't saying goodbye. She'd gotten exactly what she'd wanted. But how long were they going to be able to keep up this friendship charade, this friendly *bet* charade, without getting seriously hurt? She knew she was in more danger than he was, but still.

"Jake…"

"Alice…"

She stared up at him. This was all part of the game, that friendly bet. It wouldn't be enough for him to just lean down and kiss her. She had to be the one to kiss him. She had to be in control of this, driving it. Putting on the brakes if she wanted to. Or firing up the rocket boosters. Her choice.

The power of that choice was dizzying.

She locked her knees in place to keep from swaying. Maybe he was a bad kisser. It was possible. Maybe he'd have some weird nibbling fetish, or it'd be too wet or too dry. Kissing him might actually help matters some, by taking him down a few notches in her brain. Who knew?

And now, all of a sudden, she *did* need the bathroom. She'd always had a nervous bladder.

She took a deep breath. What she hoped looked like a patient breath. "Okay. *One* kiss. As an experiment. And to get you to shut up about it."

His lips tilted at that. He wasn't buying it. But whatever.

He leaned even closer, until his breath puffed warm and soft on her mouth. He smelled minty. He reached casually over and grabbed the bookmark rack behind her shoulder. She let her gaze flick to his considerable bicep and how the plaid shirt stretched over it.

"I'm ready when you are, darlin'."

And there were those eyes again. She felt like she was being drawn into the mother ship. He was pulling her right on in, and she was powerless against it. *Kiss me.* Okay. *Fall in love with me.* Don't mind if I do…

Her poor heart slammed against her rib cage as she reminded herself that she wasn't, in fact, powerless here. She was holding all the cards, even though it didn't feel like it. She could duck right under his arm and make a beeline for the bathroom, and he'd be the one wondering what the hell happened. But she didn't want to. She guessed because she was a glutton for punishment. And she kind of liked the fact that despite the senior-football-hero look on his face, there was a genuine look of desire, too. He wanted this just as much as she did, and it didn't *really* have to do with a bet made over birthday tequila shots.

Okay. She'd kiss him. But she wasn't going to let herself fall any deeper than she already had.

"Sometime this millennium, Bloom?" he asked, his voice maddeningly smooth.

God. She wanted to pop him right in that mouth. And she also wanted to trace his bottom lip with her tongue.

She'd just have to settle for somewhere in between. Standing on her tiptoes, she leaned in to give him a quick peck on the lips. But bumped him in the nose instead. Hard.

He hadn't even had time to pucker. He rubbed his nose and leaned away.

"Seriously?" he said.

"Well, I was nervous!"

"That was *not* a kiss. That was a baseball bat to the sinuses."

Her cheeks caught fire. "I'm sorry I'm not as used to this as you are. You probably kiss someone every other day, for God's sake."

He smiled at that. "Well, not *every* other day."

Groaning, she pushed him aside. "If you don't mind, nature calls."

"I have a feeling you don't really have to go. You just want to run away from me."

"Bingo."

"What if I promise next time will be different?"

He reached out and touched her arm, stopping her. She turned, more embarrassed than she'd been in a long time. She remembered feeling this way in high school a lot. It was like those recurring dreams where you showed up to class in your underwear. That's always how Alice felt. Like she was the butt of a joke, only she could never figure out just what she'd done to make people laugh.

To be fair, Jake wasn't laughing. He was teasing her good-naturedly. But in Alice's mind, at this exact moment, she couldn't really distinguish one from the other. It was humiliating to be this nervous around a man. She knew how to kiss, of course. But he didn't know that.

"What?" she bit out, unable to keep the wobble from her voice.

His expression was uncharacteristically tender. "We can do better than that."

"We?"

"I'm part of this equation, too. I take full responsibility

for my nose being in the way."

She rolled her eyes, but felt her mouth tug into the beginnings of a smile. "I'm actually a good kisser, you know."

"Oh, I don't doubt it."

"And I *was* nervous."

"Me too."

"Liar."

"Should we try again?" he asked, his voice low. "What if I meet you halfway this time?"

Her stomach curled into a warm little ball. It definitely felt like they were in a bedroom now. But it was still a bookstore. The teenage girl in the next aisle over blew a bubble and snapped it with alarming precision. The lady in the American flag sweatshirt gave her a withering look.

Reaching out, Jake brushed Alice's cheekbone with the backs of his knuckles. He wasn't smiling anymore, and she was suddenly breathless.

"I want it on record that I'm tackling a pretty significant fear right now," she whispered.

"Whatever you say…"

He leaned down slowly, and she could see herself in his eyes. They were the color of honey, or warm caramel. They reminded her of all things good and sweet. And slightly forbidden.

She felt his breath again, puffing on her lips. But this time, she didn't fight it. Pushing away all logic warning her she was the worst kind of fool, she leaned into him with her heart wide open. She'd pick herself up and dust herself off later. Right now, she just wanted his mouth on hers. To know what that felt like.

Jake settled his hands on her hips. She was shaking, but was barely aware of it anymore. Maybe trembling was just going to be part of the experience where Jake was concerned. Like doing things that were out of character—like going to the bar on Saturday nights and dancing to Keith Urban.

Letting him hold her still, she closed her eyes and felt her lips part slightly. Her blood rushed through her veins like a swollen river in the spring. She could hear it swooshing in her ears, threatening to carry her away if she'd let it.

"It's okay," he whispered. "I've got you."

And then his mouth was on hers. Alice had only lost time once in her life, and that's when she'd found out her mother had died. She'd almost fainted that day. She remembered the world spinning, spinning, and reaching her arms out to try and steady herself before she fell. Kissing Jake was kind of like that.

Only without the heartache.

Chapter Ten

A LICE WALKED BESIDE her dad up the gently sloping hill of Eastwood Cemetery, Marietta's oldest, and in Alice's opinion, most beautiful resting place. It was listed on the National Register of Historic Places, so it was naturally a source of deep local pride. There were even a few gunfighters buried here, shot by someone faster during Marietta's copper mining days toward the end of the 1800s.

She breathed deeply the sweet scent of Montana's native wild flowers that were sprinkled over the hillside like confetti, and looked around. She imagined the cemetery probably looked much like it had over a hundred years ago when there were only a few plots marked by wooden crosses. Giant evergreens towered over the graves, creating a natural canopy from Montana's harshest weather. The grass wasn't emerald green and perfectly manicured here like at the cemetery across town near St. James church, but rather growing in stubborn tufts—prairie grass that was tough as the mountain soil it took root in. This was where Ava Bloom had wanted to be buried. So it was here that she rested, underneath a beautiful, gnarled oak tree, and beside a simple marker that read, *Always In Our Hearts*.

Alice's dad huffed a little beside her as they made their way up the hill, but hadn't said much since getting out of the car. He was like this every visit, quiet and lost in his thoughts until they reached her mom's grave to lay down her favorite flowers—a small bouquet of white lilies. And then he'd start talking. Asking Alice about herself, things he might've been missing in their day-to-day routine at the funeral home. They'd actually had some of their best talks on this hill. It was here where she'd finally forgiven him for keeping her mother's illness from her. And here where she'd told him she wanted to go into the family business. She didn't think he'd ever looked so proud.

She loved their visits to the old oak though, because talking beside her mom's grave felt like a way of keeping her close. And Alice imagined that she might be able to hear them from where she was. And she might even be happy where she was. At least, that's what Alice liked to think.

As they neared the top of the hill, her dad slowed, and then stopped, looking out over the small town nestled below. The sun had just peeked its golden head over Copper Mountain, and lovely rays of light were beginning to filter through the tree branches overhead. Early morning bugs flitted around, but the bees were still asleep, lazy and non-committal in their kingdom of blooms.

"You know, I'm not sure golf is doing the trick any-more," her dad breathed, planting his hands on his hips. "I might have to supplement with some cardio."

Alice put her hands on her hips, too. "We could start running. I think there's going to be a 5k benefiting Marietta

General this fall. We could do it together?"

Her dad smiled, his breathing starting to slow some. "You'd want to do that with your old man?"

"Of course! And I think Mom would've liked it, too."

"You're right, honey. She would've."

They stood there for a minute, listening to a few squirrels chattering in the distance. The cemetery was tranquil, still. They always made it a point to come out on mornings like these, when most of the world was still dreaming.

They began walking again, toward the oak and the pretty stone marker. Alice carried the flowers this time, a bouquet from Sweet Pea Flowers. Its heavy fragrance filled the air and mixed with the scent of pine and wild flowers.

They slowed as they reached the grave, and Alice bent to tuck the lilies at the base of the marker.

"Hi, Mama," she said.

Her dad wrapped an arm around her, and all of a sudden, she was twelve again. The painful age where most of the girls Alice knew were pushing their mothers away. She'd been desperate to hold on to hers. But her dad had done his best. He'd navigated her through school dances, her first period, her prom, and packing up for college. But she'd never stopped longing for her mom. For her sweet and steady presence in her life. As wonderful as her dad had been, it was impossible to fill that deep, dark void inside her. And Alice knew it would remain empty until the day she died.

"You'd be proud of this one, Ava," her dad said, his voice hoarse. "She's a good kid."

She smiled. Sometimes Alice felt frozen in time where

her dad was concerned. She'd always be on the verge of becoming a teenager to him. She'd always have those skinny legs, and a permanent crop of zits across her forehead. She guessed that's what death did—it stopped the clock where your heart most wanted to be.

They stood there together, looking down at the marker. Letting the feelings wash over them in waves. There was nothing else to do but let them churn and rise, and then, finally, recede again.

After a few minutes, her dad cleared his throat and stepped away. He put his hands in his pockets and turned to her, his eyes misty. "So, how are you doing, sweetheart? Everything going okay?"

"I'm good, Dad. Things are good."

"And how's Dana?" he asked. "She seems a little down lately. A little blue, but maybe that's just me."

"It's not just you. She's okay. But she's got some things going on at home that are complicated."

"Oh?"

"Her mom wants her to come back to Wisconsin to visit, but she and her dad aren't speaking."

"Why not?"

"From what she says, I don't think he can accept that she's gay."

He stared at her. "Gay..."

She waited, letting this sink in. Dana had never said anything to him, but why would she? It had never come up.

"Dana's gay?" he asked.

She nodded.

"Oh…I didn't know."

"I think her dad said some things he can't take back, and she's having a hard time forgiving him. She's in some pain right now. That's why she's been quiet."

Her dad shook his head. He hated seeing anyone struggle—always wanting to help, even if he was a little clumsy about it. "I had no idea. I wish she felt like she could talk to me."

"She hasn't had the best track record with parents, Dad. She might be afraid of being judged."

"Well, that's ridiculous. I'm proud of her. She's family."

Alice smiled. That was her dad. All in, all the time. "I know she'd appreciate that. She thinks a lot of you."

"I think a lot of her. I wish she'd stop putting holes in her face, but…"

Alice laughed.

"How about you?" he asked. "You haven't mentioned Jake since coffee the other morning, and I got the feeling there was more to the story there." He raised his bushy brows. "Anything you want to talk about? I know it's not the same with me as it would've been with your mom, and you'd be calling her about these things…"

"Aww, Dad."

He was right. She and her mom had a special bond. And Alice definitely would've told her about Jake, asked for her opinion and advice. She longed for it, even now. But the truth was, she didn't know how to talk to her father about this, because she didn't know herself what was happening between them.

There was a part of her, the part that had slipped on the green dress the other night, that longed to be brave, fearless. Like Jake. He inspired her, made her want to stretch her wings and see if they'd carry her away. But there was also a part that was hesitant. Because she knew how it felt to be hurt by circumstances, by people. Even well-meaning people had the power to cause great heartache, and she didn't want to feel heartache right now. She wanted to be happy. Confident in her career and relationships. She felt like she'd finally hit her stride at the funeral home, even thinking of teaching a Modern Funeral Practices class at the community college in Bozeman that winter. And a fling with a bull rider who'd probably leave a trail of scorched earth in his wake would only get in the way.

"I'm right, aren't I?" her dad said, watching her. "About there being more the story?"

She looked down at her sneakers, dusty from the walk up the hill, and kicked at a pebble. It went bouncing away like a rubber ball. "I don't know. Kind of. Yes."

"Which is it?"

"Yes, there's more to the story. Only I don't know what it is yet. I like him. Is that crazy?"

"Why would that be crazy?"

"He's this rodeo star. Bigger than life. And I'm...you know. Me."

Her dad frowned. "You never give yourself enough credit. Your mom would say the same if she were here."

"Dad..."

"Don't Dad, me."

It was best not to argue. He was protective of her, and was in a certain amount of denial that she'd been as lonesome as she had been growing up. But just when she thought he'd buried that part of her adolescence altogether, he'd mention something—a painful memory that she harbored, too. And she knew he got it. He just didn't like to go there.

"You're amazing, Alice," he continued, his voice low. "Inside and out. You could hold your own with anyone if you wanted. But the question is, do you want to?"

That was the million-dollar question. She chewed the inside of her cheek and gazed out over the cemetery. It looked so pretty this morning in the dappled sunlight. The sky was changing from a burnt orange to a rich, honey yellow. Soon, it'd be as blue and wide as the ocean, the marshmallow clouds sailing across its great expanse.

"I don't know, Dad," she said. "I really don't. I want to do things like follow my heart. But I want to be smart about it, too. When do you choose one over the other?"

He shook his head. "Oh, sugar. I wish I knew the answer to that. I wish I had some good advice for you, but I'm not sure what to say."

They stood there on the hill beside her mother's grave, quiet then. Listening to the soft sounds of nature around them. Feeling the warmth of the sun on their shoulders.

And then, in the distance, there was a rustling in the bushes. They turned to see a deer stepping into the morning light. It was a doe—her eyes big and dark, her fur a deep, textured taupe. She stared at them, while her small tail flitted back and forth. She was clearly deciding if they were a danger or not.

Alice and her dad stood absolutely still, not wanting to scare her away.

After a few seconds, the doe relaxed, lowering her head to nibble at a flower. And then out stepped a tiny, spotted fawn behind her.

"Oh," whispered her dad. "Oh, look at that."

The baby's huge ears rotated back and forth like fur-lined radars. And then it lifted its glistening black nose to test the air. They all watched each other in silence. In wariness. But after a minute, the wariness faded, and a delicate trust began to settle in its place.

The doe started grazing in earnest, and the baby stepped close, butting its little head under her belly to nurse. It was maybe the most precious thing Alice had ever seen.

"It's a sign," her dad said softly. "A sign from your mom. She's always watching over you, sweetheart."

With a lump in her throat, Alice watched the mother and baby, their love, their bond clearly evident in the way they moved. It was a natural wonder, what they were witnessing. Life, in all its simple beauty, was holding hands with death in all its finite complication here in this cemetery. And it was lovely to behold.

Was her mom watching over her? Alice thought she might be able to feel her in that moment, in the gentle gasp of wind through the pines above. In the flick of the fawn's tail. In the low buzz of the bees, who were just now stretching and yawning, and starting their day.

But if she was there, it was impossible to tell what her

opinion was. Alice felt her eyes fill with tears, something that had been happening at the most unexpected moments since she was twelve years old. Was she telling her daughter to be smart, guarded, like the mother deer with the wary eyes?

Or was she saying to live like someone left the gate open, like the little fawn who was just now kicking up its tiny black hooves next to its mother. In the wild flowers that grew so heartily in a place of sorrow.

Chapter Eleven

J AKE SHRUGGED HIS shirt back on, wincing at the familiar pain in his shoulder. His physical therapist, a snowboarder in his mid-thirties, who was also a fellow adrenaline junkie, stood leaning against the door with his arms crossed over his chest. If anyone could understand why Jake loved rodeo, it was EJ Corpa. Which was why the look on the other man's slightly sunburned face now was so irritating.

"We should be further along by now," EJ said, his voice even. He was probably expecting an argument. Which he wasn't going to get. Jake was in a damn good mood today. And he was finding that denial was surprisingly easy to embrace if you worked hard enough at it.

"I think it's starting to feel a little better, actually. Those exercises are doing the trick."

EJ watched him.

"Besides," Jake continued, "Copper Mountain isn't until the end of September. We've got plenty of time."

The other man nodded, the muscles in his jaw working back and forth. "Yeah, well… I'm not worried so much about getting you back on a bull, as what will happen to that shoulder once you're in the middle of riding one."

Jake began buttoning his shirt, doing his best to ignore that. A timer went off in the other room. An obnoxious reminder that some poor schmuck was done with one torture session, and ready to embark on the next.

"I know you hate these conversations," EJ said.

"I get it. You're only doing your job, man."

"Well, part of me doing my job is to advise you about this injury. And not only this injury, but all the injuries you've walked in here with."

"I've had a few. So have you."

EJ's mouth tilted knowingly. "I'll admit to that. But I do try and minimize the wear and tear on my body. The risk to it. You're limited to what you can do on the back of a two-thousand-pound animal."

"That number's inflated. More like fifteen hundred."

"I'm telling you, another dislocation in that joint, and you're looking at surgery, Jake. And there's no coming back from that."

"I can always learn to ride left-handed." That was a stretch. But he detested feeling like he didn't have a choice.

"I need you to think about what I'm saying. Can you do that for me?"

"Sure."

Jake slid off the massage table, his boots hitting the floor with a thud. He could smell coffee from the break room and his stomach growled.

"Has anyone ever told you you're incredibly stubborn?" EJ asked.

Jake ran a hand through his hair. "Every damn day."

"And how's that been working out for you?"

"Pretty well. Up until now."

"You do know there's life after rodeo, right?"

Now the guy was starting to sound like Jenny. Yeah, he knew there was life after rodeo. But he wasn't ready for it yet. All of a sudden, he pictured Alice. Lovely Alice. Would she be as attracted to him if he was just a normal guy with a nine-to-five job? She thought she wanted someone who didn't take the risks he did. But what if the risks were all part of the draw?

It didn't matter. It really didn't, because he couldn't wrap his mind around retiring yet. There had been so many girls who'd asked him to. Becky for one. And none of them had given him a good enough reason.

Pushing away Alice's image, and the memory of her full, giving lips, he grabbed his hat off the hook by the door. "I know," he said. "I know there's life after rodeo. I'm not interested in that kind of life right now."

"Then, when? When you're too broken to enjoy it?"

EJ had fixed him up a lot over the years. They were more friends now than anything else. And that was precisely why he was getting away with pushing the issue now. Anyone else, and Jake would've been out the door five minutes ago.

Instead, he stood there looking down at his hat, pinching the brim between his fingers. He took a full breath, felt it saturate his lungs, before looking back up again. "I don't know how *not* to rodeo, man," he said. "I really don't."

EJ put his hands in the pockets of his khaki slacks, and watched him. There was a muted voice outside the closed door, telling someone that it was okay, they could do ten more. The smell of coffee wasn't making Jake hungry anymore. It was turning his stomach. EJ was right. He hated these talks.

"Why?" EJ asked, his voice low.

Jake shrugged, looking out the window to the denim-blue mountains in the distance. *Why?* It was a hard question to answer, because it was equally hard to be honest, even with himself. He wasn't used to honesty when it came to rodeo. He was used to making it through from one injury to the next. Gutting it out, no matter the cost. But these last few weeks had been different. And he wasn't sure why. It'd be easy to say it was Alice, and the way she looked at him, like she believed there was more to him than what he chose to show the world. But it went deeper than that. Jake was having to face his future, and who was he if he wasn't riding bulls? If he wasn't proving to everyone who cared that he'd damn sure die with his boots on?

EJ had said he was stubborn. But Jake wasn't just stubborn. He was scared to death that what Alice saw was nothing but a perfect illusion.

Why? The question seemed to reverberate in his heart, over and over again until he wondered when the breaking point would be.

He jammed his hat onto his head, pushing it down low over his eyes. "Too many reasons to count, partner," he said.

"HELLO," ALICE SAID, shaking the woman's hand, and holding it just a few seconds longer than she normally would've. But she couldn't help it. This was a person who looked broken. Fundamentally. "Please let us know if you need anything, Mrs. Dougherty. We're here for you."

Jill Dougherty, a petite woman in her mid-forties, dabbed at her red, chapped nose, and nodded. Her eyes were glassy. She was somewhere else. Somewhere Alice couldn't follow.

Pulling her hand back, she let her husband escort her into the flower-filled chapel where people were starting to file slowly in.

This would be a big service. The deceased wasn't an elderly person today, or someone whose death had been expected in any way. It was a college student, killed while cliff jumping over the Flathead River.

Alice swallowed hard as Dana came to stand next to her. The guests were all so young. Some of them looked like they'd come straight from the lake themselves, with scattered freckles across their sun-kissed faces.

It was wrong, burying someone who'd had such a bright future. But the service pamphlet wasn't apologetic. Instead, there was music that he'd loved, pictures of outdoor conquests, poems that celebrated living life to its fullest. And a list of all the adventures that he'd had in his twenty years.

So many. So many dangerous hobbies, that Alice felt a stab of unexpected anger before she could help it. His mother was in agony, and would never be the same again. His friends, it seemed, hadn't learned anything, except that life was disposable. And this young man with so much ahead of him was about to be buried, his very being extinguished as easily as a candle being snuffed out. And for what? Ten seconds of free-falling through a bright blue sky?

She shook her head and looked away. It wasn't her place to feel anger. It was her place to offer comfort and love. And if this life was taken too early, she wasn't in any place to judge. Still, in her heart, she couldn't help but see the similarities to what Jake was doing. How fast he could be killed, taken from his family and friends. For nothing. For a gold belt buckle, prize money, and bragging rights. She couldn't understand it. She didn't want to understand it. She wanted to walk away from him and all his high and mighty ideas of what a career should look like, and never look back. Only now, she'd kissed him. And now, it was going to get messy.

Dana glanced over. She could feel her friend's steady gaze, but didn't return it. She was having too hard a time not crying on the spot, which wasn't like her. Whatever else Alice was, she was a consummate professional. She always held it together at funerals.

"You okay?"

"I'm fine," she said. *Lie.* She wasn't. But Dana didn't have to know that.

"This one is hard."

She nodded, looking at the large, framed picture of Hunter Dougherty at the front of the room. In it, he was laughing, shirtless, holding a rafting paddle above his head triumphantly. Droplets of water were suspended in the air around him, frozen in time for all eternity.

"I don't understand it," Alice whispered. "Why? When he had so much to live for?"

"But that's what he was doing. Living."

She bit her lip. A little too hard. She wished she could see it like that. It was how Jake saw it. It was how a lot of people saw it. But she just couldn't. She loved too much, wanted to hold her friends and family too tight. She'd always thought people like Hunter were selfish. But maybe she was the selfish one.

"I admire him," Dana said softly. Maybe a little wistfully. "He wasn't afraid."

It was impossible to argue with that, as Alice gazed at the photo of the kid in the raft. "No, he wasn't," she said. "He wasn't afraid."

They were quiet then, as people continued taking their seats. There was no organist today. Instead, folk-acoustic music played over the speakers, something buoyant and sweet. Goose bumps popped up along Alice's bare arms as a young girl laid an evergreen wreath in front of Hunter's picture. She didn't look a day over eighteen. Probably wasn't. Tears streamed down the girl's cheeks as she took a seat next to his mother. She didn't bother wiping them away.

Alice's father walked up beside them. He smelled like aftershave, looked dapper in his black suit.

"Alice, will you turn down the air?" he asked. "It's warm in here."

Dana slid her a look.

"Okay, Dad."

"And, Dana…"

Her friend turned, raising a dark, pierced brow. All three of them stood in a somber line, shoulders almost touching, their expressions similar. They really were a team, Alice thought. Sometime in the last six months, they'd become a quirky little family.

"I just want you to know I think you're a wonderful young lady," her dad said. "And I'm proud of you."

It was totally out of the blue. Almost comical in how out of the blue it was. And just when Alice worried the moment couldn't get any more awkward, her dad went ahead and pulled Dana into a bear hug. Just like that.

Her friend stood stiff for a second, unwilling to yield. Maybe afraid to be loved for who she was. Or afraid to admit she might need that unconditional love, which was the scariest thing of all.

But then, she raised her thin arms, slowly, hesitantly, and wrapped them around Alice's father's neck. They stood there, hugging it out, and didn't even look awkward doing it. Somehow, it fit.

Dana's shoulders shook a little. Alice couldn't be sure, but she thought her tough-as-nails friend might be crying.

Again.

Chapter Twelve

J AKE GLANCED OVER his shoulder. "Which way?"

"Turn left!" She had to shout through the helmet, and pointed for good measure. "That way!"

He nodded, and revved the Harley's engine at the stoplight. The roar reverberated in Alice's chest, made her heart pound with the beginnings of excitement, even though she willed it not to.

Still, she hugged him tightly around the middle, reveling in his body, hard against hers. It was hot today, and the sun beat down on her shoulders, burning them pink. She should've worn a T-shirt at least, but hadn't been thinking straight. Jake had that effect. She was on a motorcycle, after all—Exhibit A.

When the light turned green, he eased through the intersection and continued down Main Street past the Java Café, and Big Z Hardware and Lumber where people were walking through the parking lot, carrying their bags. She wondered if anyone recognized her on the back of the big bike. Probably not. She felt like someone else, completely incognito behind the glossy black helmet that smelled a little like sweat, and a lot like man. It was kind of thrilling to feel like someone else.

Like she had permission to enjoy this until they got where they were going. Or until they crashed into a tree. Either, or.

She looked over Jake's shoulder toward Eastwood Cemetery. He didn't know yet that's where they were heading. Their friendly bet had mentioned walking through a park to stop and smell the roses. She'd been kind of vague about the definition of the word park, and whether or not the roses would actually be attached to a bush when they got there. Details, that as far as she was concerned, didn't matter. The point was to take him to a place he wouldn't normally have gone himself. And he definitely didn't seem like a cemetery kind of guy.

But there was something inside her that wanted him to see this place the way she did. Not full of sadness, but full of beauty. Not a place of loneliness, but a place where the living came to remember, to feel the presence of their loved ones, and to feel the loneliness slip away, if only for a few hours at a time. But most of all, she wanted him to see where her mom was at rest. That part was becoming important to her, even if he ended up thinking she was off her nut for bringing him out here. It was worth the risk. They'd kissed, and that meant something, no matter how hard she was trying to convince herself otherwise.

They slowed at the stop sign on 5th Street, the big bike idling at the empty intersection. Jake put his foot down to balance them. "Where are we going?" he yelled back at her. "The park by the fire station is back there."

She pointed straight ahead. He followed her finger toward the hills in the distance, and the brown historical marker that read *Eastwood Cemetery, est. 1892, Marietta, Montana.*

He stared at it. "That's not a park, Alice."

"I know!" she yelled back through the helmet. Probably a little too loud, but her voice sounded like she had her head in one of those cones they put dogs in to prevent post-surgery licking. "It's prettier than a park. You'll see!"

She could only make out the side of his face, but he looked skeptical. This was it. A moment of truth. Maybe he'd finally be turned off by her love of all things morbid. At least, that's what other people would probably think of spending time in a cemetery for the scenery.

Swallowing down the cotton ball in her throat, she grasped his T-shirt in her fists, as he revved the engine and accelerated through the intersection, toward the narrow dirt road that led to the cemetery.

They passed the old, iron gate, welcoming them with its rusty arms open wide. Hundreds of pink and yellow wild flowers bobbed a hello, as the long, wispy grass on the hill bent to the will of the insistent breeze. Jake eased the bike toward a turnout under the shade of fragrant spruce, and cut the engine.

Waiting for her to climb off the back, he lowered the kickstand and smiled as she pulled the helmet off. "A cemetery, huh?"

"It's not just any cemetery," she said, running her fingers through her hair. "It's a historic cemetery. Haven't you ever walked through one just to look at the markers?"

"Negative."

"Well, then." She handed over the helmet and smiled back. "I'm dying to see what you think."

"Was that a joke?"

"Do you want it to be?"

"It was kind of funny."

"Then, yes. It was."

"Ha. Ha."

He hung the helmet on one of the handlebars, swung his long leg over the bike, and stood to stretch. His T-shirt rode up, exposing his abdomen, along with a line of dark hair that ran down to disappear behind his worn leather belt.

She looked away. But not fast enough. He grinned wickedly as he lowered his arms to his sides again.

"Aren't the flowers gorgeous?" she said quickly, hoping to distract him. "The pink ones over there are called Fuzzy-tongued Penstemon. And there's some Scarlet Paintbrush. The bees love those."

He wasn't looking at the flowers. He was looking at her. And his gaze was no match for the blazing sun overhead.

She chewed the inside of her cheek and studied her sneakers.

"So," he said. "You come here often?"

"Pretty often. I was just here with my dad."

"For a funeral?"

She hadn't gone into details about her mom yet. And suddenly she felt like a book that was about to be opened to the very middle page—where someone had pressed a delicate flower to dry. It was a tender, vulnerable moment, and she wondered for a few seconds what she was doing here with this cowboy, who had the ability to crush that flower between his fingers and scatter the broken pieces into the Montana wind.

"My mom's funeral, actually," she said. "And every month since."

She looked up then. He was looking back. And everything she'd thought she'd known about Jake Elliott was lost in that moment to the very same wind she'd been wary of. The look on his face wasn't one of pity, like she absolutely expected. After all, she was a woman in her mid-thirties who'd never been able to move on. At least not in what most people would call a normal way. Instead, she thought she saw something close to admiration in his eyes. Which was strange, because Alice didn't really think of herself as admirable. She went about her days just like everyone else. Except, unlike everyone else, she was afraid of what those days might bring. Death, for one. A broken heart, for another. And maybe a random airborne illness thrown in for good measure. But admirable? *Nope.*

Even so, that wide mouth of his curved softly, in such a way that said she wasn't too far off. When she'd met him that night at the Wolf Den, she would've found it difficult to come up with anything about Jake that was soft. His body was hard, his attitude was hard, his head was *extra* hard. But here he was, standing in one of her favorite spots, smiling at her like a gentle giant. And he would've laughed at that, but that's how she saw him right then. Gentle, above all else. And that tough-guy bull rider routine? She knew it wasn't an act. But that wasn't all he had going on, either.

"You've come here every month since your mom died?" he asked.

She nodded.

"Your mom was a lucky lady to have been loved so much."

"She was a good mom."

They stood there for a long moment, listening to the sound of the breeze through the branches overhead. The spruce shivered slightly, sending a few needles raining down around them.

"My mom wasn't around much," Jake said, looking over at the hill where the grave stones, some over a century old, stood stoically in the afternoon sun. "After my brother's accident, she pulled away from us. I know it was a defense mechanism, a way for her to survive it. But it still sucked. Not having her there. Emotionally."

For the first time, Alice was able to picture him as a boy, trying to negotiate childhood on a farm with a big, complicated family. She could understand why he might want to push the envelope with rodeo. Maybe as a cry for attention. Maybe to prove to himself and to everyone else that he could take his licks and then some. It made sense.

"Have you ever talked to her about it?" Alice asked. She half expected him to shut her down. But now that the door was open a crack, she was desperate to get a look inside.

"My mother doesn't do heart-to-hearts. Not her style."

"She might feel differently now. Time has a way of softening people, even if they have a hard time showing it."

"No, she's still pretty much as distant as ever."

"I'm sure she's just worried about you, Jake. Maybe it's that defense mechanism working overtime."

He shrugged, putting his hands in his pockets. His expression was shuttered now. She'd hit a nerve.

"We don't have to talk about it," she said softly.

"I don't mind talking about it."

"That's not what your body language says."

"What does my body language say?"

"It says shut up."

He smiled. Relaxed his shoulders a little. He was trying. "I don't usually talk about it. But I don't mind talking about it with you."

"Can I ask you a question?"

"Shoot."

"Does it bother you that people you care about don't embrace your career?"

He kicked at the gravel with his boot, sending up a small cloud of dust. "Maybe it used to. At the beginning. But I don't like to think about things like that when I rodeo. You think what I do is dangerous? Just watch a cowboy ride when he's distracted over a woman or family or kids. *That's* dangerous."

"So you like to stay unattached because it makes you a better bull rider."

He thought about that for a few seconds. "Maybe. Maybe that's true."

"Don't you ever get lonely?"

He looked at her steadily. Practically looked right through her. Again, she wondered if he'd had enough. She was pushing, and she knew it.

"Sure," he finally said, his voice even. "Sure, I get lonely."

She stood there, absorbing what he'd just said. He'd just admitted something she was pretty sure he'd spent most of his adult years denying. In fact, she wasn't altogether sure she'd heard him right.

"You look shocked," he said. "Why?"

"Because...you act like you don't need anyone."

"Needing and wanting are two different things, Bloom."

She thought about all the women who must follow him around endlessly. There was a void they weren't filling. A place inside him they weren't touching. The question was, would he ever let anyone get close enough to try?

"What about you?" he asked, stepping closer. "Are you lonely?"

She grazed her bottom lip with her teeth. *That* was a loaded question. It was more like, *how* lonely are you, Alice? On a scale of one to ten.

"I think I've always been lonely. But I'm used to it. It's my jam."

He smiled, reaching out to tug on a strand of her hair. She found herself staring up at his mouth before she realized what she was doing and forced her gaze away.

"Now, from where I'm standing," he said, "I find that hard to believe."

"Why?"

"Because you're so fun to be with. You're pretty as a damn picture. And you're funny. Has anyone ever told you that?"

She frowned. There was that kid in second period gym class. But now that she thought about it, she couldn't remember if he'd said funny, or funny-looking. It didn't matter. At the moment, it felt like her heart was going to beat right out of her chest.

"How's a woman like you lonely?" he asked, stepping even closer. Another few inches and he'd be brushing up against her. It was all she could do not to arch her back.

"I think you know the answer to that," she said. "You're just being sweet."

He rolled his eyes. "Christ. I'm not sweet. Don't you know me at all by now?"

"Oh, I think you're very sweet. I think you like to hide it behind that cocky cowboy thing."

"Well, then you're the only one."

"I have a theory about you."

"Oh, really. Let's hear it."

"I'm *not* the only one. I think women are attracted to that sweetness. They sense it. I don't know that it's the cocky cowboy thing at all that they like. Not really."

He looked amused. He stared down at her, his lips tilted. "So your theory is that my secret weapon is sweetness."

"Yup."

"Huh."

"I'm not saying you're all sweetness all the time. But, you know. It's there. Deep down."

"I'll never look at myself the same way again."

"It's good to have insight."

"What happens when I turn out to be an ass, Alice? When I push you away like I've pushed everyone else away for rodeo? Then what?"

She swallowed hard. Okay, so clearly he already had some insight. Maybe he didn't need her minor in psychology to help him out here.

"Doesn't mean you're not sweet," she said, looking him straight in the eyes. "It just means you're conflicted."

"Oh, I am. Very conflicted."

"Told you."

"Because I really want to go to bed with you. And I also want you to leave me alone, so I don't fall any harder than I already have."

Alice felt that like a punch to the stomach. All of it. He was falling for her? Well, that went against all the laws of nature as she knew them. She was supposed to be the one falling for him. And then, yes. He'd end up pushing her away, and she'd have to nurse a severely pummeled heart. Her head was spinning.

"You do?" she managed.

"Well, *yeah*. Why do you think I haven't kissed you again? Why do you think I didn't drag you into a corner in that bookstore and give all the other customers an R-rated peep show? Because I'm conflicted, Alice."

"But you're here with me now. Why are you agreeing to all these outings?"

"Because I'm also competitive as hell, and this is a real bet we've got going on. I wasn't kidding when I said I was going to get you skinny-dipping."

She stared up at him. The wind whispered through the tree overhead, through the prairie grass and flowers surrounding them. The cemetery felt like it had been waiting for them, like it wanted to stay still, so it could hear the pounding of their hearts.

Jake's eyes grew dark. Serious. Brooding. And it worked for him. All of it.

"You know what?" he said, his voice low. "Screw it."

Sliding an arm around her waist, he pulled her close. She went because she was hungry. Hungry for everything she'd been denying herself for so long. Love, adventure, heartbreak. Because with heartbreak came feeling. And that was better than being numb. Than being afraid all the time.

He lowered his head and kissed her. He tasted minty, smelled like soap. But it was how he felt that was making it hard to breathe.

She parted her lips and he accepted the invitation. He pressed himself against her and she reveled in the cold, hard contours of his ever-present belt buckle. Of his hips and thighs, which were thick and muscular against her own.

He slipped his tongue inside her mouth, as she moved her hands up his arms, exploring him. His faded gray T-shirt strained against his biceps, his skin hot to the touch. Everything about Jake was hot. Hot and blistering as a newborn star.

She felt his big hand move across her lower back. Then lower, over the swell of her butt. He squeezed gently, and she heard herself whimper as she pushed herself against him. She couldn't help it. She wanted more. Needed more.

So it made sense that Jake was the one to break the kiss. She wouldn't have been able to. Not on a bet.

He pulled away, moving her hair away from her face. She was dizzy, unsteady on her feet. *This must be what jumping out of a plane feels like,* she thought. *Or bungee jumping off that bridge over the river...* She felt like she was falling through the air, waiting for something or someone to catch her. It was terrifying.

"You're scared of flying," he said. "Right?"

She watched him, having trouble processing. "What?"

"You told me that first night you were afraid to fly. It was on your list of things."

"Oh. Right. Yes, afraid to fly."

"What do you say to kicking another one of those fears to the curb?"

"If you're talking about skydiving, you're nuts."

"One thing at a time, Bloom. Do you like baseball?"

She smiled. "Uh…"

"Do you like baseball? I want to take you to a baseball game. In Chicago. The White Sox."

"You want to fly to Chicago for a baseball game." She had to repeat it to make sure she'd heard him right.

"Why not? Once I'm back on the circuit, it'll be a while before I can catch a game again."

Her stomach sank at that. It was silly, because he hadn't given her any indication that he wasn't going back to rodeo. Of course he was going back. But the words were like a bucket of ice water over her head. A shock to the system. An unwanted reality check. What was she doing again? Oh, that's right. Falling in love with a guy who had no intention of settling down or leaving his killer job for her. Ever.

She shook her head. She couldn't think straight. It was the heat. Or the kiss. Or both. "I don't…"

"We can stay overnight, have some deep-dish pizza, be back the next morning. And I promise to keep my hands off you."

She looked up at him.

"Okay," he said. "*Mostly* I promise to keep my hands off you."

"Didn't you just say you were conflicted?"

"Yes, but this is all part of living in the moment, darlin'."

He wasn't playing fair at all. He must know when he called her that, her knees went weak. Literally. It was hard to form a coherent thought, let alone make a decision that might leave her broken in a few weeks' time. This was becoming more than just a harmless bet, a game between the two of them, and she knew it.

"I have work… It's been busy lately…"

"Can't Dana cover for you?"

She could, that was true. There was nothing at the funeral home now that Dana couldn't handle. And Alice knew her friend would approve of this little adventure. She'd been pushing her toward the idea of Jake ever since her birthday.

"She can…"

He smiled slowly, looking like he'd already won. Like he'd conquered something—a challenge he was up against. Was she just a challenge for him? There was always that possibility. He could be saying all the right things, things he

143

knew she wanted to hear, in order to get her into that lake. In order to get her into bed. She railed against the thought, at the same time as she accepted it as reality. Sex was a reward that men like Jake would work for to a certain extent. Love, most likely, wasn't. And in his world of living fast and dangerous, the lines were probably forever blurred.

"The bet has been fun," she said, suddenly more confused, more wary than she'd been since meeting him. "It's been good for me in so many ways. But I don't know that this is a good idea, Jake."

"You're thinking too much."

"You're not thinking at all. We're supposed to be friends."

He sighed. "Your words, not mine."

"You don't want to be friends?"

"Sure, yeah. But there's no reason why we can't be more. Have some fun."

"In theory, that's great. In theory, that's why I came out to the Wolf Den that night to find you. In *theory*, nobody gets hurt."

"I'm not going to hurt you, Alice."

"How can you say that? You can't promise anything, and I'm not asking you to. But don't you think it'd be foolish of us to take this to another level knowing how it's going to end? I know a part of you does. You just admitted it."

"Yeah, but I kissed you anyway. And neither one of us knows how it'll end."

"I can guess."

"Jesus, woman. Can't you just take things as they come

for once?"

A lump rose in her throat that she willed back down again. He sounded frustrated. And she was frustrated with herself. And she was irritated with him. This wasn't how this beautiful day was supposed to go. They were supposed to be smelling the roses, for crap's sake.

"Like you take them as they come?" she bit out.

"Sure. Just like that."

"Speaking of foolish…"

He frowned. "What's that supposed to mean?"

"What do you think? You know how I feel about the risks you take. It's none of my business, but it applies here."

"Alice," he said, his voice sounding strained. "You can't control every single thing in your life. You're going to die. I'm going to die. You're going to get hurt. We're all going to fall at one point or another, but what can you do? You get back up again. You deal with it. You go on."

"I know. But you're so blasé about everything, Jake. You and me? That's a big deal. At least for me it is. Why would I risk it?"

His hazel eyes flashed. She was getting under his skin. But she was only pointing out the obvious. She couldn't believe he wasn't seeing it.

"Why?" he asked. "Because of what we talked about the night we met. Or have you forgotten about that already? Because it seemed like you were wanting to start taking some risks then."

"You want me to be like you. I'm not like you. I'll never be like you, and I don't think you can accept that as part of the reality of this relationship…friendship. Whatever."

Now he looked mad. But she raised her chin. This was his fault anyway. If he hadn't taken a shot with her that night, none of this would've happened. She would've shaken his hand at the funeral, admired his butt from a distance, and that would have been it. Instead, she was staring him down as if she were some kind of girlfriend. As if they were on the verge of having a fight, only to make up between the sheets or something.

"You think I want you to be like me?" he bit out. "That's what this is all about?"

She crossed her arms over her chest.

"Why the hell would I want you to be like me, Alice?" he said. "I'm selfish, shallow, arrogant. I know this about myself. I'm not proud of it. I'm attracted to you because you're *you*. And, yeah. I'd love it if you'd let loose, but only because I want you to see how that feels. Like you want me to see how sniffing books feels."

She opened her mouth to say something, but clamped it shut again. She wasn't sure what she wanted to say anyway. She didn't know how to argue with Jake, because he always seemed to know how she felt better than she did. He definitely knew all the right things to say. Things that made her heart melt right along with her underwear.

"A baseball game is just a baseball game," he continued softly. "No hidden agenda, except maybe to get you on a plane. And into my lap for a few minutes."

She laughed, unable to help it. "At least you're honest."

"Hell, I'm trying to be. But you make everything so

hard."

"I told you I'm not easy."

"I'm beginning to see that."

"But you still want to take me to a baseball game. In Chicago."

"Damn straight," he said, taking her hand. "And I'll even bring anti-bacterial wipes for the seats."

"A man after my own heart."

"Saturday, then?"

The wind moved her hair against her face. The cemetery was quiet, peaceful. There was no doe here today, and no fawn hiding in the brush. No sign of her mother watching over her from another world. Just the stillness of a summer afternoon and this man standing in front of her, who was turning out to be the biggest unknown of her adult life. He wasn't promising her anything but a good time. And no matter what she'd just said, she really did want to be like him. To have a good time without thinking things to death.

"Saturday," she said.

And wondered what she'd just gotten herself into.

Chapter Thirteen

JAKE WALKED DOWN the aisle of Marietta Western Wear looking at the crisp white shirts, their price tags spinning in the air conditioning. He hated shopping. But Copper Mountain Rodeo was coming up, and he was due for some new clothes. He was just vain enough to want to play it up for the crowd, who always made a big deal out of his pretty-boy looks. Although the female fans were a little further from his mind than usual. Today, he was only thinking of one in particular, and wondering if she'd even show up to see him ride.

Jesse was browsing through the hats on the wall. His brother was taller than Jake, and wiry, where Jake was thick and muscular. But the resemblance was hard to ignore. They had the same strong features, the same strawberry blond hair. The same smile, although they'd be hard-pressed to admit it.

"What do you think of this one?" Jesse asked, jamming a black cowboy hat onto his head. He usually wore white, like Jake.

"Fine. If you're going for Johnny Cash."

Jesse studied himself in the mirror. "Not bad. Not bad at all, if I do say so myself."

"And humble, too."

"You should talk. Mr. *I've got a spec of manure on this shirt, so I'll go out and buy three more.*"

"Whatever."

Jesse put the hat back on its hook. "If I have to hear one more hot girl asking if you're single, I'm gonna puke."

"As long as it's not on my new shirt."

As if on cue, a young brunette walked by and lowered her lashes at Jake. He smiled back. None of this was lost on Jesse, who groaned in the next aisle over.

Jake shrugged, picking up a shirt and checking the tag for the size. Something by Hank Williams was playing through the speakers overhead, and the entire place smelled like leather. If he absolutely had to shop, it was less painful here, where most everyone knew who he was. He could milk the celebrity thing, which annoyed his brother to no end, and depending on who was working the register, sometimes he even got a discount. It was entertaining. Although, he had to admit, without Jesse there to rub his nose in it, it was decidedly less fun. Today was one of the good days.

"Speaking of," Jesse said, coming up next to him, "I heard you were out with your funeral home director again."

"My *funeral home director*?"

Jesse nodded.

"She has a name. It's Alice."

"I heard you were out with *Alice* again."

"Word travels fast."

"You got her on the back of your bike?"

"Who said that?"

"Only everyone in town."

Jake rubbed the back of his neck.

"So?" Jesse asked, eyeing him.

"So what? Nothing to tell."

"Bullshit."

"We're just hanging out."

"Naked?"

"What? *No.*" It was normal for Jesse to be all up in his business. It was normal for him to rib Jake, and vice versa. But for some reason, he wanted to keep this part of his life private, and that was new. It was delicate, an unknown. And he didn't necessarily want it dissected by his brother. Or anyone else, for that matter.

"Come on, Jake. You don't *hang out* with anyone, and you know it."

"What are you getting at?"

"Oh, shit. Like you don't know."

Jake grit his teeth and picked up another shirt.

"You're kind of an ass when it comes to the ladies, brother," Jesse said. "You've said it yourself."

"Only because I don't want to get married? You've been talking to Jenny too much."

"No, because you plow through them like candy. I mean, I don't blame you. You've got them lining up. But this one is different."

"Different how?" He didn't really need an answer. He knew Alice was different. Fundamentally. And that's what bothered him.

"She's not your type."

"Christ. Okay, Dr. Phil. What's my type?"

"Blonde. Curvy. Experienced. Curvy…"

"Am I that shallow?" He didn't need an answer to that, either.

Jesse hooked his thumbs in his pockets. "Jenny's right. I asked around. She seems like a nice lady."

"You asked around? Good God."

"I'm just saying. You know that poor kid who was killed a few weeks ago? The Dougherty kid? She and her dad helped pay for the funeral."

Jake looked over at his brother.

"Yeah," Jesse continued. "The family was having a hard time coming up with the money, so the Blooms took over." Jesse snapped his fingers. "Just like that."

"Huh…"

"Like I said. Nice lady. You should really cut her loose if you're not interested. That'd be the decent thing to do."

Jake prickled. And maybe that was because he'd thought of doing the exact same thing. But for some reason, he was having a hard time pulling the pin.

"Since when are you the voice of reason when it comes to women?" he bit out.

"Since I had lunch with Jenny a few days ago."

"Knew it." Jake walked over to the hats and plucked one off the hook. It was brown and ugly as sin, but he couldn't have cared less. It was something to do with his hands.

"She's got a point," Jesse said. "It wouldn't kill you to settle down. Start thinking about other people for once. You're almost thirty."

"Are you serious?"

Jesse shrugged. He was a little old lady. Next, he was going to be knitting Jake booties and telling him to take his vitamins.

"Thanks for the advice," Jake said, "but I'm fine."

"Whatever you say."

"Whatever you say," Jake muttered under his breath.

"I'd rethink that one." Jesse nodded at the hat. "You look like hell in brown."

Jake stared at his brother, incredulous.

"Jake?"

They both turned at the sound of a female voice behind them. There, holding a black leather purse with the Marietta Western Wear tags dangling from it, was Alice's friend from the funeral home.

She smiled, looking young and beautiful under the soft store lighting. The various diamond and silver studs in her face sparkled and flashed. She reminded him of some sort of pixie from a children's book.

Jake smiled back. "Dana, right?"

"That's right."

"This is my brother Jesse."

Jesse stepped forward and shook her hand. "Ma'am."

Her gaze shifted from Jesse back to Jake again. It was sharp, knowing. "I recognized you, so I thought I'd come say hello."

"Glad you did," Jake said. "We were just..." He looked down at the hat in his hand and made a face before putting it back on the hook. "Browsing."

"Brown isn't his color," Jesse offered up.

Dana laughed. "I'm sure he'd make it work."

"How are things at the funeral home?" Jake asked, feeling the need to steer the conversation away from his clothing choices. You never knew what was going to come flying out of his brother's pie hole. Next, it might be something about his recent shift from tighty-whities to boxer-briefs.

"Good, they're good. I mean, as good as things can be at a funeral home."

"What do you do there?" Jesse asked.

"I'm an embalmer," Dana replied, gazing at him steadily. It was obvious she was used to a certain kind of reaction. And from what Alice had said, people could be idiots when it came explaining the funeral home business to them, which didn't surprise Jake any. He knew a lot of idiots.

But Jesse, bless him, didn't skip a beat. "That's cool. Must be interesting."

"It is. Sad sometimes, for sure. But interesting. Anatomy fascinates me, so…"

They all nodded, Jake trying not to think about the specific ins and outs of that comment. He'd flunked biology in high school. Dissecting a frog hadn't turned out to be his strong suit.

"You know, I couldn't help but overhear Alice's name," Dana said.

"Oh…" Jake glanced at Jesse who had an infuriatingly juvenile look on his face. His brother delighted in awkward moments like these. Because he was basically twelve.

"I'm sorry," she continued. "I didn't mean to put you on

the spot. And I know it's not my place…she'd actually kill me if she knew I'd said anything. But she thinks the world of you, Jake. Really."

He looked down at her, a familiar feeling beginning to press in on all sides. It was the instinct to move on before anything got too complicated, too serious. It was what had kept Jake on his toes all these years. What had kept him sharp, focused. Staying on the backs of the nastiest bulls for eight seconds, with room to spare.

But there was another feeling, too. It was a boyish excitement stirring in his gut. It was as new and unfamiliar to him as a baby's first cry. And it was taking him off-guard.

He swallowed, shifting on his feet. "I think the world of her, too," he said. "She's…" He tried to think of something that would encompass what he truly thought of Alice. Things that went beyond her looks and her quirkiness and her pluck. But it was hard to grasp on to anything because there was so much to her. He didn't know where to start, what to say in the middle of this store, with his brother standing right there, and the hokey country music serenading them in the background.

"Great…" he finally finished lamely. "She's really great."

Dana watched him, her expression unreadable. Then she took a measured step forward. Then another, until she was standing right in front of him. All five-foot nothing of her. She tilted her head back and stared up at him, narrowing her heavily lined eyes.

All of a sudden, he wanted to move away. She looked like a bobcat who'd stopped purring and had gone very still.

"Good," she said, her voice low and raspy as an old Hollywood starlet's. "That's good. Because she's a wonderful person who deserves all the kindness and love. And if you hurt her, I'll personally craft your balls into a Christmas ornament to sell at my neighbor's church bazaar."

Jake stared at her.

She smiled sweetly, and patted his chest. "Have a nice day, fellas."

He watched her walk toward the register, shocked into silence. When he'd recovered enough to look over at his brother, Jesse was smirking. Of course he was.

"See?" Jesse said. "Told ya."

Chapter Fourteen

ALICE SAT IN the window seat of the private Cessna with her stomach in her throat. They were waiting in line to taxi, the sun glinting off the wings of the plane like shards of gold. It was a beautiful day—deep blue sky, puffball clouds, a light, north-northwesterly breeze that Judd Harlow, their pilot, said would move them along to Chicago a little faster.

Alice didn't care about getting there faster. She only cared about getting there in one piece. She felt like she was going to be sick.

Jake, for his part, sat beside her dozing, of all things. He had his head back against the seat, his eyes closed, a lazy tilt to his lips. *Jackass.*

She poked him in the thigh. "Hey."

He looked down his nose at her. "What?"

"This doesn't bother you at all?" She was honestly having a hard time remembering why she'd agreed to this.

"Nope."

"Well, you can't *sleep* through it."

"Why not? It's good sleeping."

"Jake."

He smiled and sat up. "Okay. I'm awake. It'll be fine."

"Says who?"

"Thousands of planes take off and land every day. Statistically, it's much safer than driving."

"Statistically. But at least in a car, you have a chance. In this thing…" She tapped her window. "I'd feel better if parachutes were mandatory."

"Then you'd be skydiving. One step at a time, Bloom."

She groaned, but leaned closer into Jake's warmth as the plane lurched forward. She'd only flown once before, and that had been as a kid to visit relatives in Denver. The only thing she remembered was an alarm going off about five minutes after takeoff. The flight attendants had explained it was from something burning in the kitchen, but she'd never forgotten the terrified look on her mother's face, and the way she'd clutched Alice's hand for an hour afterwards.

Their family had driven everywhere after that, and as a result, she'd never been east of the Mississippi. She longed to travel, but like with everything else, she'd been letting fear dictate that, too. Which was why going to this godforsaken baseball game was such a big deal. It was a first. In a growing line of firsts. She had Jake to thank for that. And Jake to curse for it, too.

He put an arm around her shoulders, and she turned her face into his neck as the plane picked up speed down the runway. His collar smelled like aftershave.

He held her close, breathing into her hair. Her belly curled into a tight little knot, her pulse skipping erratically in her wrists, as the small plane lifted into the air like a bird. The engines hummed outside the Cessna's windows as it climbed and banked gently west.

Jake leaned close to her temple. She squeezed her eyes shut and dug her fingers into this thigh.

"You're missing the view," he said, softly.

"I'm good."

"Open them for me? Just for a minute?"

Swallowing hard, she opened one eye. Then the other.

"Atta girl. Look to your left. We're flying over Sleigh Bell right now."

She did as she was told, but didn't let go of his leg. Didn't lean away from his neck. Just turned her head enough to see the lovely Victorian house and red barn on the hillside. She could make out the tiny dots of horses grazing in the pastures, a pickup truck driving down the lane and kicking up a cloud of dust behind it.

"Oh…" she breathed.

"Have you ever been on a horse before?"

"Not unless you count the ponies at the fair."

"I'm thinking something a little more exciting."

"Or dangerous."

"That, too."

She watched as the farm slipped from the window like a memory. And then they were in the clouds, the sun filtering in through the windows and warming her bare legs a little. Her chest felt tight. She'd gone through a horse phase like a lot of little girls, but the furthest she'd ever gotten were posters on her walls and reading every single *Black Stallion* book Walter Farley had ever written. And now, here she was. Sitting beside a handsome cowboy, on the verge of him teaching her how to ride.

She ran her tongue over her lips, and wondered with a pang if that would ever happen. As the weeks passed, and as Copper Mountain Rodeo got closer, so did Alice's feeling of dread. Would she be saying goodbye to Jake when his shoulder finally healed? When the newness wore off this latest adventure of his? This latest challenge? Or worse, would he start riding again and leave her to watch him get hurt, or even killed, from the sidelines of his heart?

Even as a friend, if that's what she was to him, she would feel that pain to her very bones. She struggled against this new desire she felt, and the intense need to protect herself at all costs. It was a constant storm churning inside her, and it was wearing her down. Just for the weekend, just for the next twenty-four hours, she didn't want to think about the consequences of anything for once. She just wanted to live in the moment. If they'd ever get off this damn plane alive, that is.

Jake put two fingers underneath her chin, and turned her head back to where she faced him again.

"I know I promised to keep my hands off you." His gaze fell to the V-neck of her white cotton T-shirt, which was riding low enough to expose the swell of her breasts. When he looked back up, his eyes were dark. "But I really want to kiss you right now."

She stared up at him. Sometime in the last few seconds, she'd forgotten all about the plane, the baseball game, her fear of large crowds. And she felt her lips part slightly. She wanted to be kissed.

"I'll take that as a yes," he said. And leaned in the rest of the way.

They'd kissed before. Twice to be exact. And both times had left her trembling in her boots. But this time... This time was hungrier. Less gentle. More raw.

His tongue flicked against hers as she opened her mouth wider. Her stomach, which had been in a knot before, curled in a warm ball of yearning and anticipation.

He slipped his hand underneath her arm, and splayed it against her rib cage. His thumb stroked the side of her breast, making her nipples strain against the thin cups of her bra.

Her pulse hammered behind her ear, at the hollow of her throat. And she thanked God she was sitting, because she was pretty sure she'd be swaying otherwise.

After a few more seconds, he caught her bottom lip lightly between his teeth, teasing her for one ovary-bursting moment, before pulling away again.

"You okay?"

It was only then that she realized her eyes were still closed. And they were on a plane. And the elderly gentleman sitting across from them, reading his newspaper, had probably witnessed the whole thing.

Slowly, she opened her eyes. He was smiling at her. Like he knew something she didn't.

She smiled back. "Yeah. Yeah, I'm okay."

"How are we doing with the flying thing? Hanging in there?"

"I'm doing..." She was doing fine. More than fine, really. If she'd known that kissing an insanely hot guy at fifteen thousand feet would be all it would take to cure her fear of flying, she'd probably have gone to Italy right after college. "I'm all right," she finished. "Thanks."

Jake looked at his watch. "Should be there before noon. That'll give us enough time to get checked in and grab a quick bite before we head to the game. Excited?"

"I am. I've never been to a baseball game before."

"*Ah.* Don't want to hear it. La la la."

"I'm just saying, I—"

He put a finger to her lips. "I've never dated a girl who hasn't loved baseball. Ever."

Her heart slowed in her chest. *Oh, God.* What did that mean? Were they dating? Or was she looking for signs that weren't there because she liked him so much? This was a date. For sure it was. But one date and *dating* were two different things. Dating meant keeping a toothbrush at his place. It meant sex on Saturday nights after dinner and a movie. It meant holding his hand in public and getting to tell him she was terrified that he rode bulls for a living, and having him listen and take her fears into account.

She smiled as he took his finger away, but her expression was forced. Because if dating meant getting him to listen to her fears, the real ones, the ones that truly mattered, then she was out of luck.

She didn't think Jake Elliott would listen to anyone.

LOWER LEVEL. TWO rows up. Behind the dugout. Close enough to see the spit flying from the catcher's mouth, and the stitching on the ball. Jake didn't think he'd ever gotten better seats in his life, and he had Lucky to thank for them. His girlfriend was a local podcaster who had some connections, and as it turned out, she knew people who knew people. Her last guest had been the sister of a White Sox outfielder. And that was that.

Leaning back, he adjusted his dark aviators and took a long, slow drink of beer from his plastic cup. Then glanced over at Alice, and smiled.

She looked beautiful. Of course she did, because that was Alice through and through. But she also looked completely adorable with her brand-new White Sox cap turned around backwards. It was too big, and ended up covering the tips of her ears, too. He'd bought her a huge, spongy finger, which she was currently waving in the air. She'd been waving it after every word from the announcer. After every whistle from every fan sitting within a two-mile radius. And as it turned out, she had an impressive set of lungs on her, too. Anderson had hit a homer at the top of the third, and she'd hollered like an honest-to-goodness baseball fan right then. He'd never been more proud.

Setting the giant sponge finger in her lap, she took another drink of her wine, and smiled back at him. She'd put sunscreen on before they'd gotten out of their Uber, but her nose was still pink. Along with her cheeks and her chest. He doubted she ever saw this much sun. But it looked good on her. More than good. It looked healthy, vital. The alcohol was probably responsible for part of that flush, but still. It was working. All of it. And Jake couldn't take his eyes off her.

"What?" she asked.

"Nothing. You. I think you might be headed toward a little sunburn there."

"Oh…" She looked down at her chest and pressed her finger to her skin. It left a white spot that slowly turned red again. "Oops."

"Are you hot? Uncomfortable?"

She shook her head. "Nope."

"Alice."

"What."

"Are you buzzed?"

"Nope. Nooooo. I'm great. I love baseball."

He laughed. "Okay. Maybe we should have some water next. Just to keep you hydrated."

She looked down at her chest again. "I forgot. I'm also afraid of melanoma. And alcohol poisoning."

"Seems reasonable."

"But this is the new me. Tackling things I'm afraid of. Flying, skin cancers, you…"

Okay. She was definitely buzzed. Adorable. But buzzed.

"I don't think you've tackled me yet. I'd remember that."

She grinned and took another sip of wine. Then tapped him on the arm. "*You*, sir, are a lady killer."

"I wouldn't go that far."

"I would."

The player who was up to bat, number forty-two, swung

and missed. The entire crowd let out a collective, *aww…*

"Popcorn!" a vendor in a blue smock yelled a few feet away. "Get your popcorn here!"

Jake leaned over Alice, and caught her scent. Shampoo, mixed with the tangy, sweet scent of warm skin and deodorant. "One water, please."

The vendor took Jake's five and tossed him a bottle in one fluid motion born from hours of practice.

"Keep the change, man."

The guy nodded, then headed up the stairs again. "Popcorn! Get your popcorn here!"

Jake unscrewed the top and handed it to Alice. "Drink a little or you're gonna have a headache with all this sun. Trust me."

She put the bottle to her lips, and took a long swallow before handing it back again.

"You know, I think I have to go to the bathroom," she said matter-of-factly.

"Okay. Want me to go with you?"

"I think I can handle that part on my own." She winked. "But thanks."

He watched her stand. Then sway.

"You know what?" she said, touching her temple. "I'm a little dizzy. Maybe you should come. In case I fall over or something."

"You got it."

Standing, he took her hand. They made their way down the aisle, trying not to step on people's toes as they went. Alice wrapped her fingers around his, and it felt as natural as anything he'd ever done, holding her hand. It felt domestic and warm, and there was something about it that was comforting in a way. Weird word, but it was the one that came to mind. Jake was so used to doing everything on his own, convincing everyone in his life that he didn't need them, that he never stopped to actually enjoy their presence. And when he was with Alice, he enjoyed everything about her.

As they walked up the steps toward the bathroom, the late summer sun warm on their shoulders, he wondered just how long he'd feel this way. Wondered when the instinct to run would overpower everything else. It had been rearing its head for a few weeks now. Blustering like an angry bull. But he'd been pushing it to the back of his mind, to the outer corners of his heart, in order to get closer to Alice.

He clenched his jaw as she walked beside him, her arm rubbing against his, and he knew she'd been right all along. It was stupid to be playing this game. Because there were very real consequences for the loser. She didn't want to get hurt—she'd been clear about that. And he didn't want to be the one to hurt her. And yet, here they were. In the city, drunk, or close to it, with their hotel only a few blocks away. He was an asshole.

"Oh, my God," she said, pointing to the bathroom. "The line."

He looked up. It stretched out the door and around the corner. All kinds of women in White Sox gear, waiting wearily, some holding the hands of little kids doing the potty dance.

"Uh, how bad do you have to go?"

She took off her hat and ran a hand through her hair. "Well, I've had two glasses of wine. Plus some water at your insistence. So…pretty bad."

At the same time, their gazes shifted to the men's bathroom, where predictably, the line was non-existent. A steady stream of men walked in and out, blissfully unaware of the female fans next door whose bladders were all close to popping.

"You know," he said, "you *could…*"

She stared at him. "No. No way."

"Why not? It's not like you'd get carted off by the baseball police. You gotta go, you gotta go."

She chewed her bottom lip, processing this. Probably deciding how close she was to wetting her pants. She looked back at the line stretching out the women's bathroom door and frowned.

"You're a wild woman now, Alice," he said, elbowing her in the side. "You *flew* here."

"You're right. I did do that."

"And you forgot to use hand sanitizer before you ate your hotdog."

"Oh, gross. I did forget, didn't I?"

He grabbed her hat and jammed it back on her head. "You got this, Bloom. Let's see what you're made of."

She gazed back at him. Her cheeks were definitely sunburned, and tiny new freckles were scattered haphazardly across her nose like confetti. "Just like bungee jumping, right?"

"Well, no. But whatever."

Lifting her chin, she ran her hands over her shorts like she was smoothing a cocktail dress. "When you gotta go, you gotta go," she said. "I'll be right back."

He watched as she marched toward the bathroom, head held high, unapologetic.

Rubbing the back of his neck, he smiled. The Alice he'd met in the Wolf Den last month would probably have chosen to grab a taxi back to the hotel before using the men's restroom in a baseball stadium. But he was slowly starting to see that the Alice he'd met last month, and the Alice who was probably sashaying right past a urinal that very minute, were two different people. This bet had been ridiculous from the start, he'd own up to that. It had been a way to get to know her better. To kiss her and maybe get to second base if he was lucky. He hadn't taken it seriously. Not really. But here she was—turning everything he knew about her, everything he knew about himself, on its ear. And he wasn't sure how he felt about that.

After a long minute, she appeared in the doorway of the bathroom, smiling from ear to ear. "I did it!" she mouthed.

He grinned. She absolutely did.

Chapter Fifteen

ALICE FOLLOWED JAKE through the doors of the Hyatt Regency, her head spinning. She looked up at the sparkling chandelier in the lobby, and couldn't really be sure there weren't two of them. Or three.

Jake glanced back at her. "You good?" He'd been fussing over her since leaving the game, which was sweet. She was fine. In fact, she was more than fine. She didn't think she'd ever had so much fun in her life.

That third glass of wine at the bottom of the seventh probably hadn't been the best idea. But she'd been sure to drink lots of water with it. Honestly, she thought most of her lightheadedness was because of the sun. And the fact that she needed to eat something more than ballpark franks.

"I'm fine," she said. "Honest."

When he turned back around to wait for the lobby elevator, she let her gaze drop to his butt. Nobody had a nicer butt than Jake Elliott. He had the hottest buns in Marietta. In all of Chicago, for that matter. Even those baseball players with the tight uniforms and even tighter glutes had nothing on Jake.

All of a sudden, she wondered what it would feel like to

press herself against him. To wrap her arms around his waist and feel his solid backside against her stomach. It wasn't exactly the first time she'd imagined it, but it was the first time she'd had the urge to actually do it. Dancing had been one thing. Kissing, another. But they were in a hotel now, spending the night. And yeah, they'd gotten separate rooms, but still.

Alice ran her tongue over her lips, tasting the salt there. The grittiness from a full day in the heat. Jake stood with one hand planted on the wall, the other on his hip, and stared down at his boots as they waited for the elevator. She wondered what he would do if she came up behind him and slid her arms around him. Would they go directly to his room? Tear each other's clothes off in a frenzy of passion? Or would it be slower? More deliberate? A reveling in each other's bodies that would take some time to get just right.

A couple walked past, talking in low tones and holding each other tight. Jake slid them a look, his face expressionless. Alice watched them with a sudden rush of envy that surprised her. She wanted that, too. But at what cost? Jake would come with a high price, she knew that. She'd accepted it a long time ago.

Only tonight, something had made her go numb. Maybe it was the alcohol. Or maybe it was the sun zapping her of any remaining common sense. But tonight she was less afraid, and more turned on than anything else. Not just drawn to his body, which most women would be, but drawn to the man himself. The unexpected tenderness, where there should've been only rough edges. The way he made her feel safe. The way he was bringing out a whole new side to her. She wondered what her mom would've thought of Jake. But really, she could answer her own question—her mom would've loved him, because of how Alice felt about him. Simple as that.

The elevator dinged and the door opened. Jake turned and motioned her in before walking in after her. He punched the third-floor button and stood quietly, unusually quiet, as the door whispered shut again.

Pulling at a loose string on her cutoffs, she studied the back of his neck. His skin was smooth and tan, like saddle leather. Strawberry blond stubble pricked his jaw, and she wanted to know exactly how that would feel against her softest, darkest places. She wanted to be touching him. She wanted to be running her fingertips along the planes of his broad shoulders. She wanted to be naked with him, feeling the hotel's crisp, cool sheets sliding underneath them.

She lowered her head. These were not the thoughts of someone who was afraid, and weighing the consequences. These were the thoughts of a woman who'd been given a small, savory taste, and was hungry for more.

The elevator came to a stop and the silence between them was almost deafening before the door finally opened with another ding. An elderly woman stepped in as they stepped out, smiling a toothy smile.

"Ma'am," Jake nodded as the door closed again.

Alice's heart squeezed. She never thought she'd be falling for a cowboy. A Harley-riding, womanizing, panty-busting charmer. But here she was. Loving him just like everyone else. What the hell kind of chance did she stand against the entire female population of the world, anyway?

Don't answer that, she thought, as they made their way down the hall, their feet silent on the cushy carpet.

Jake reached into his back pocket and pulled out his key card.

She realized she was shaking. Just that minute was aware of it. As if her body had finally caught up to her brain and was getting a clue. She'd made up her mind in the lobby. She didn't want to go to her own room. She didn't want to play it safe.

He turned, his face still expressionless. A blank canvas that she couldn't read.

"You sure you're okay?" he asked. "Still dizzy?"

She shook her head. She wasn't dizzy. Or maybe she was, but her libido wasn't having it.

He tapped the key card against his thigh, watching her. It was impossible to tell what he was thinking. But the fact that he wasn't leaning in for a kiss, even a goodnight one, made her eyes burn.

"Probably wouldn't hurt to have more water when you get to your room," he said. "I know my way around hangovers, believe me."

When you get to your room... He wasn't planning on jumping her bones. He wasn't even planning on taking her bra off with his teeth. He was going to be a complete and total gentleman, dammit. She rocked forward on the toes of her sneakers, and back again, holding his rich, hazel gaze.

Then, with her pulse racing, she stepped forward. Then

closer. Close enough to put both hands on his chest. "I was thinking…"

He watched her. But didn't touch her. Didn't move an inch.

"I was thinking," she continued, "that maybe I shouldn't sleep in my room tonight." The words eased over her vocal cords like honey on warm toast. Easier to say than she'd expected. Maybe she was a wild woman after all. At least where Jake was concerned. Who knew?

A second passed. Then two. Then he wrapped each of her wrists in his big hands, and slowly lowered them to her waist.

"Alice…"

Her throat began to ache. *Uh-oh.* She'd lost her ever-loving mind. He was about to break her heart into a thousand sparkly shards.

"What?" she managed.

"I want to. I want to more than I can explain right now."

"Then don't explain anything," she said. "We don't have to talk. We don't have to figure out if it's a good idea or not."

"I know it's not a good idea."

She watched him. "I don't care."

He raised his brows.

"I don't," she repeated. "This is something I want. We both want it, you just said."

"I know I did."

"Then let's…" She didn't know how to finish that sentence. *Get naked* was what immediately came to mind.

"You're drunk," he said, his voice low.

"I am not!"

"Alice."

"Maybe a little buzzed. But that's it. Scout's honor."

"What if you want to kill me in the morning? What if you regret it?"

She pressed herself against him, surprising herself. Again. "I won't regret it."

He shook his head and took a step back. He looked frustrated. To prove it, he shoved a hand through his hair, making it stick straight up. "Dammit, Alice. I'm not really used to being a decent guy, and I'm trying to be."

"I never asked you to be anything you're not."

"See? Now that's bullshit."

She planted her hands on her hips. "What?"

"You never asked me to be anything I'm not. That's true. Not out loud, at least. But I know you don't like what I do for a living. And if we sleep together, and this gets any more complicated than it already has, then what? I'll have to start weighing those worries of yours. And, Jesus. I sound like my grandma here. I hate that I sound like my grandma." He scowled at her. "I never used to care about the consequences of anything. When I planned this trip, I wasn't that concerned about them. But the problem with you is you're making me think about things I normally wouldn't. You're making me feel guilty. And I don't do guilt."

"So, you're blaming me for being thoughtful?"

"Yeah. I guess I am."

"Well, that's not my fault, Jake Elliott," she bit out.

"Sounds like you've got some things to work out."

"Sounds like I do."

They were both scowling now. Her ears were hot. She'd practically thrown herself at him, and he was rejecting her for all the right reasons. She couldn't be mad at that. But she was. She was so confused, she couldn't even think straight anymore. He was supposed to be taking her shorts off right that minute. Instead, they were having an epic lover's spat in the hallway of the Hyatt Regency, that wasn't really a lover's spat at all, because they weren't lovers, bless it.

He sighed, his broad chest rising and falling slowly. Then his expression softened some. "The truth is, I'm starting to care about you. And frankly, that makes me want to split."

She frowned. "At least you're being honest."

"I don't know what's wrong with me. I've never had a problem with lying before. At least not about feelings and shit."

"Feelings and shit," she mumbled, trying not to smile. She was too mad.

"The truth also is," he said, "you deserve someone better than me. Someone who'll be safe and careful, and who'll be around for the long haul to take care of you."

She couldn't stay mad. He was making it impossible. "I don't need anyone to take care of me." But even as she said it, she knew that was kind of a lie. Speaking of lies. She didn't *need* anyone. But at the same time, she'd always craved the closeness, the security, of a relationship. She longed to be someone's love. And to have a love of her own. She wanted what her parents had. Affection, desire, longevity. The whole package, and Jake was right. He probably wasn't the guy who'd be able to deliver all that. And it wasn't fair to ask.

She raised her chin. Stopping short of stomping her foot. "This is just sex, Jake. Just sex, not love. I'm not asking for anything more."

His mouth parted slightly. It was obvious she'd taken him off guard. That was okay. She'd taken herself off guard.

His eyes heated slowly, surely, as the words, the meaning of them began to sink in. "You're not one-night-stand type, Alice. I don't know a ton, but I know that much."

"I didn't used to be. But maybe I am now."

"No." He shook his head. "Nope."

"You know I've changed these last couple of months. You know it."

"You've gotten bolder," he said. "You haven't gotten dumber."

"Sleeping with you would not be dumb."

"It wouldn't be one of your best ideas."

"I can take care of myself." Okay. Talking him into it was turning out to be a little convenient. It wasn't allowing her to think deeply about what he was saying. Which made a lot of sense. But she didn't want to be making sense. She wanted to be showering with him.

He reached out and cupped her cheek. She closed her eyes and leaned into his hand. His thumb moved over her cheekbone, and was so gentle, she almost forgot what he did for a living. Almost forgot that he was right—she'd never be able to put the bull riding aside. It would always be between them, no matter how mind-blowing the sex turned out to be. And she had no doubt that it would blow her mind.

She opened her eyes again to see him watching her. All this would be so much easier if she wasn't falling in love with him. She was. She absolutely was, and that was making it ten times worse. She was really trying to be the kind of woman she knew he preferred. The uncomplicated kind. The fun kind. She wanted that, too. But her dumb heart kept getting in the way.

"What if at the end of the day, we're just too different?" she asked, a sudden lump in her throat. She didn't explain, but she knew she didn't have to. Like him, she guessed she'd known it all along, but hadn't let herself think it, truly, until just now. The idea of not being with Jake, in one form or another, was almost too much to bear. But the idea of being with him, and then losing him was worse. And that's what he'd been trying to tell her. In his own way.

He pulled her close, and wrapped her in his arms. She laid her cheek against his chest and felt his heart thudding there, strong and sure. He smelled like Jake. His own unique scent that never failed to set butterflies loose in her lower belly.

"You know," he said, moving his lips against her hair. "The bitch of it is that I like you too much for you to hate me."

"I'd never hate you."

He chuckled softly. "You've never been in a relationship with me. You'd hate me. And I don't think I could take that."

It was maybe the sweetest thing she'd ever heard. And possibly the most painful. Because it felt like he was letting her down easy. Which he absolutely was.

She pulled away enough to look up at him. "So," she said, her voice raspy. "Friends, then?"

He tucked her hair behind her ear. "Abso-freaking-lutely."

She smiled. It was hard not to.

"Which means you'll have to come see me ride," he continued. "So I can see that pretty face from the stands."

"I don't think I'll ever be able to see you ride."

"Even if I promised to go to the damn opera?"

She stared up at him, her lips parting slightly. *Well, wonders never cease...* Before she could help it, she pictured herself in the stands at the Copper Mountain Rodeo. Imagined the sharp smell of animals, the roar of the Saturday night crowd. She could almost see Jake climbing on the back of a massive bull, its muscles rippling and quivering underneath him. And then she saw the chute open, the bull exploding out in a blind rage, doing everything in its power to free itself from the man on its back.

And that's where her imagination went black. Out of necessity. Out of survival. Because she couldn't stomach the thought of Jake being thrown off, of being trampled, his neck or back being snapped. Couldn't stomach the thought of it happening right in front of her, and knowing she didn't try and do something to stop it.

She pulled in a breath and let it out slowly. The warm, floaty buzz from the wine was starting to wear off. In its place was the slightest touch of a headache at her temples. Too much sun, too much excitement, too much hopefulness. Jake thought he was invincible. Looking at life through the lens of an obstinate little boy. But the way he looked now, standing there gazing down at her, he was anything but invincible. He looked vulnerable. Very capable of being hurt. And she was more than aware, it was the one true thing he was afraid of.

"I think you're going to have to want to go to the opera, Jake," she said. "That's the beauty of it. Everything else was just part of the bet. But the opera…that has to be for you."

He nodded, seeming far away right then. Weighing what she said. Maybe imagining himself in a darkened concert hall. In a tux. Listening to the music, and hearing it with his whole heart. It'd be a sight for her sore, sore eyes. But she let that image go black, too. Because it hurt too much to let it have its way.

He cleared his throat. "More importantly, when will you let me take you to another baseball game, Bloom?"

She felt her lips stretch into a smile that threatened to break her in two. The irony was clear—if Jake was only her friend, she could have him for the long haul. And she'd take what she could get.

"Go, Sox," she said.

And stood on her tiptoes to kiss him on the cheek.

Chapter Sixteen

J AKE ROLLED OVER again, trying to get comfortable. It was only 12:30, but felt like it should be dawn. The shrill cry of a siren on the streets below made him wince and turn his face into his pillow. And then it passed, a police car, or fire truck, or ambulance, heading who knew where, leaving the room quiet again. Too quiet.

Sighing, he flipped back over to stare at the ceiling. He wondered if Alice was sleeping. Probably. Why wouldn't she be? She'd agreed when he'd pointed out the obvious—they weren't going to work together. No matter how you sliced it, they were just too damn different.

Moving his arm over his eyes, he tried concentrating on the soft purr of the air conditioner. The feel of the cool air against his skin. He tried not to think about what it would be like lying there next to Alice. Naked. He frowned and imagined how crappy it'd be if they'd slept together, and then he went ahead and ruined it. By being a guy. By being himself. It wasn't hard to picture. But at the same time, he wondered if it would've been worth it. Something deep inside told him it probably would've been.

This wasn't helping. He kicked the covers off, letting the

air conditioner blow over his semi-naked body. The city was hot and muggy, and the lingering effects of the beer were still pulsing through his veins. He stared at the darkened light fixture on the ceiling.

Rolling over again, he pulled a pillow to his stomach and took a deep breath. Then another. And another, until he felt himself relaxing, finally, into the cool sheets.

Jake drifted toward sleep, but was only half aware. Behind his closed lids, he was holding Alice, like he'd been wanting to all along. It wasn't the pillow he had his arms around, but her. He could smell her hair, the flowery scent coming from her skin. Feel its softness, the way it slid like silk against his.

And just as he was giving up consciousness, willingly, happily, to slip into his dream world with her, a shriek ripped him away.

He shot up in bed. Then blinked up at the fire alarm, his brain still foggy. It flashed neon white, lighting up the room in hyper, pulsing bursts. The alarm itself was so loud, it rattled his teeth.

He swung his legs over the side of the bed, and stumbled toward his clothes. There were people in the hallway. He could hear them rushing past, talking in low, panicked tones. And then, the smell of smoke…

He froze. The tangy scent burned his nose. Made his eyes sting. Took him back. He'd know it anywhere…

Pulling on his jeans and a T-shirt, he fought the rising feeling of panic inside his chest. The overwhelming urge to run. A survival instinct that was so imbedded, he didn't know how deeply until that moment. His stomach churned with it. His hands shook as he shoved his things into his bag and zipped it shut. And still, above it all, above the sick feeling unfurling inside him, was the need to get to Alice. To pull her close. To keep her safe. *Dear God, keep her safe…*

Shoving his bag underneath his arm, he opened the door to see people running down the hallway. An older couple, his arm around her, her hand over her nose. A young mother with her two kids, both in superhero pajamas. Both of them crying. She looked over at Jake as they passed, her eyes wide. They were all headed toward the staircase at the end of the hall to his left. Alice's room was to his right.

Pulling in a choking breath, he turned and made his way down the hall, careful to sidestep the people rushing by.

"This way!" someone shouted.

He watched as they ran past. Alice could be downstairs already. But he didn't know for sure, and there was no time, anyway. He had to make sure she wasn't still in her room.

Narrowing his eyes at the room numbers, he stopped when he came to hers. The door was closed. No light coming from the crack at the bottom.

He raised his fist and pounded on the door.

"Alice! Alice, are you in there?"

Before he could pound again, the door swung open. There she stood, looking confused, groggy. And scared to death.

"Jake?"

He stared down at her. Lovely, lovely Alice. *Thank Jesus.* If she hadn't answered, he would've had to find an ax to knock the door in.

He pushed past her, feeling sick, but not sick enough not to notice she was in her bra and panties. She must've read the look on his face, because she touched a self-conscious hand to her chest.

"No time for modesty," he said, flinging her suitcase open. "Put these on."

He tossed her a pair of shorts and a T-shirt as voices boomed from down the hall. People were banging on doors, ordering everyone out. A baby was crying.

"Oh my God," she said, yanking the T-shirt over her head. "What happened? I was sleeping like the dead."

"I don't know, but it's not a false alarm. There's smoke."

"I can smell it." She pulled her shorts up and jammed her feet into her shoes without socks.

Jake zipped her small suitcase up and tucked it underneath his arm with his athletic bag. "Grab your purse?"

She swiped it from the bedside table and looked around for anything else.

Grabbing her hand, he pulled her toward the door. "No time. Come on."

Outside the room, the hallway was filling with smoke. Alice put a hand over her nose and coughed. A man ran past her, shoving her in the shoulder and nearly knocking her over.

"Sorry!" he yelled, but didn't stop.

"Asshole," Jake muttered, putting an arm around her. "You okay?"

She nodded, looking up at him. A fine sheen of sweat

had broken out on his forehead, and his entire body had stiffened, tight as a drum. His voice was calm, but his eyes felt wild, searching. Searching for the way out. All he could think of was Lucky. How scared his little brother must've been that day. How scared Alice looked when she'd opened her door. And his mind churned right alongside his stomach.

Holding her close, he guided her toward the staircase. Someone had just slammed the door shut, and he fought a brief panic that it wouldn't open again. But he reached out and yanked it wide, following her through. The smoke was thicker in the stairwell, black and billowing.

"Maybe the fire is below?" she said, clutching his shirt.

He hesitated for a second, but then shook his head. He winced at the alarm shrieking next to their ears. "We can't take the elevator," he said, "and this is where everyone else went. It's thicker at the end of the hallway. We're only three stories up. We just need to get the hell out."

Not waiting for an answer, he pulled his shirt over his nose, and took her hand.

She did the same, coughing through the fabric. Tears streamed down her face as they took the stairs two by two.

And then, around the corner, came two firefighters in their black and yellow turnouts. They looked puffy and exaggerated in the small, choking space of the staircase.

They pointed down the stairs. "We've got it contained, but keep going, folks!" one of them yelled. "Did you see anyone else up there?"

"No," Jake said. "I think we were the last ones."

They nodded and pushed past, continuing up the stairs

to see for themselves.

Jake brought Alice close and they headed down the stairs, the air getting a little clearer as they went. When they got to the lobby, they pushed through the door where a group of firefighters motioned for them to keep going out the glass doors to the sidewalk.

There, people were gathered in clusters. Some bystanders, gaping with open mouths. But most were hotel guests, in pajamas, robes, and slippers. One poor woman was wearing a skimpy black slip as her husband tried in vain to keep her covered with his jacket.

A firefighter motioned for them to move. The lights from the fire engines pulsed red and blue on his face. "Folks, we need you to get back. Back up now, off the sidewalk, please."

Jake guided Alice several feet away, before putting the bags down at their feet.

Turning to her, he cupped her face in his hands. "Are you okay?"

She gazed up at him, too shocked to answer. His eyes felt less wide now, less wild. But they stung like hell.

"When I woke up and smelled the smoke," he said, his voice hoarse, "all I could think of was you. Getting to you. That was it." He smiled wearily. "One-track mind, I guess."

She swallowed noticeably. "You said you hated the smell of smoke. That your brother…"

"Yeah. Not my favorite."

"I'm sorry, Jake."

He pulled her close, and put his mouth against her temple. She smelled like shampoo. He breathed her in, his chest tight. Life was so unpredictable. It threw curve balls that could knock you out if you didn't duck fast enough. But most of all, it was short. Life was incredibly short. It was something she was fundamentally afraid of; and a mantra he embraced daily. But still, he needed reminders.

He pulled away enough to rub his thumbs over the tear tracks on her cheeks. Sometimes he could read her. Sometimes he couldn't, and found that her emotions reminded him of spring bulbs, buried underneath the surface to hopefully bloom later with enough tenderness and care. But now, at that moment, it felt like they might be thinking the same thing. That tonight was a reminder of what could be snatched away in only a matter of seconds. It was a lesson he'd learned a long time ago.

Jake shook his head, about to say just that. But decided to kiss her instead. And everything he'd been thinking then was lost to him—like the smoke that was rising into the warm night air, it vanished. Leaving only desire in its place.

THE HYATT REGENCY set their guests up in a handful of hotels right down the street, apologizing profusely for the scare, and for the inconvenience of having to stand outside on the sidewalk for an hour until the firefighters gave the all-clear.

Jake didn't mind. He was in a weird place mentally. He'd told Alice that Lucky had almost died when they were kids. But he'd left out the part where Jake would never again allow himself the weakness of getting close, of loving with all his heart, of giving any part of himself, for fear of it happening all over again. To someone else. To someone he loved. But she knew anyway.

It didn't matter. He just wanted to hold her. He'd think about the rest in the morning. Reality always came crashing down whether he wanted it to or not. The reality of his shortcomings and deep-seated fears. The reality of an uncertain future, born of a refusal to face facts. But tonight, he was going to hold her. And the consequences could suck it.

They walked down the softly lit hallway of the hotel, this one smaller and more intimate than the one they'd just left. They'd requested accommodations on the first floor. *So we can jump out the window,* Alice had said dryly. And he hadn't argued.

And this time, they'd only gotten one room. They'd looked at each other quietly as the concierge typed their info into his computer, the keys clicking through the silence of the empty lobby. But Alice's gaze never wavered. And neither had his. In fact, they couldn't seem to take their eyes off one another, as the strange feeling from earlier lingered—the desire to wrap his arms around her and keep her as close as possible.

They came to the room, where Jake stuck the key card into the lock. A green light flickered on, and he pushed the door open. The room was small, tidy. The bed was turned down and there were chocolates on the fluffy white pillows.

Alice didn't speak. Just walked across the darkened room to the window, where a crack in the floral curtains let in a sliver of light from the city.

Her face was bathed in shadow and light, her hair a dark waterfall over her shoulder. He didn't think she'd ever looked so beautiful, and that was saying something.

He put their bags down, and came up behind her. She stood as still and elegant as a doe in a meadow. How was a woman like this unmarried? Not a mother yet? Not that all women wanted that, of course, but it seemed like a natural fit for Alice. Because he knew she'd be a wonderful mother. And she'd be a wonderful wife, too.

At the thought, a tightness gripped his chest. It was a lasso, pulling his heart into unfamiliar territory. He reminded himself he didn't want to get married. He never had. And he sure as hell didn't want any sticky-fingered little kids. At least not in the foreseeable future. He wanted to rodeo. As long as he could, as long as it would have him.

Still, as he reached up and moved her hair away from her shoulder, he thought of the day in the barn, the day Lucky's mare had her foal. He thought of Jenny's scolding words about his lack of commitment, and him telling himself that was for other people. Not him. Not ever. He thought of Becky and her chubby baby, and not being able to go there, because it meant admitting maybe *wanting* to go there. Despite everything. Despite his own stubborn pride fighting him every step of the way.

He swallowed hard as she put her hand up and held on to his fingers. Maybe he'd always struggle with this. And maybe there would be regret, but later. Much later, as a lonesome middle-aged man with aching knees and a screwed-up shoulder.

Leaning in, he kissed her neck. She tilted her head to the side, and relaxed into him. They hadn't talked about what they weren't going to do, or what they *shouldn't* do, since leaving the smoking hotel. They'd been quiet, lost in their thoughts, and he was glad. In his heart, he knew what was about to happen, and he didn't have any desire to go ruining it by talking it through. To him, this was simply a way of showing Alice how he felt about her. He'd always fumbled his words, messed up declarations of love and affection. He was a clumsy man in a lot of ways. But he was not clumsy in bed. The good Lord had blessed him with good communication skills between the sheets, and he knew good and damn well Alice would leave here in the morning knowing some things definitively.

But it was more than that. And that part was harder to accept for Jake.

Slowly, Alice turned until she was facing him. The light from the sliver in the curtains cloaked her like a shroud. She looked like an angel then, sent to rescue him from himself. The moonlight, mingling with the streetlights, shone on her hair. Her moss green eyes were so dark, he saw himself in them.

Without saying a word, she stepped close and wrapped her long, slender arms around his neck. God, she was pretty. Prettier than any of the women he'd been with before—the ones from his youth who'd only cared about his status on the circuit. He'd known it then, but had told himself it didn't matter. Who gave a rip, if the end result was some good sex with no strings attached?

It was only now, with her hands in his hair, that he let himself feel the emptiness that lingered from those nights on the road. From the nights coming home to a dark house and a certain hangover. Good sex was good sex. But it didn't hold a candle to this.

He leaned down and kissed her. So tenderly at first, that he was almost embarrassed by it. Like she'd be able to tell exactly what he was thinking by the softness of his mouth.

Frustrated, he pulled her closer with a low growl in his chest. It was rougher, but she didn't seem to care. When it came to Alice, he couldn't make up his mind. Rough or soft? Slow or fast? She was everything all at once, pulling contradictions out of him like ribbon.

He could feel the hardened points of her nipples against his chest. Her hips pressed against his. And all he could think about was that night in the bar—when she couldn't even take a shot without being walked through it. She was right. She'd changed since then. The shyness, the hesitation was still there, but pushed further back, allowing something else to press forward. Her strength and will. Her fire for life, which she'd obviously been denying for a long, long time. The end result was a woman he wasn't sure he could handle, at least not with one hand on the wheel. Alice would require both hands, a whole heart, an entire promise of a future. And he knew this with an aching in his throat, even as he guided her toward the bed.

She reached for the hem of his T-shirt and pulled it up over his abdomen, over his chest, over his head. He'd wanted this ever since that first night in the bar, since turning to see her in that ridiculous blouse buttoned all the way to her chin. And Jake always got what he wanted. Always. It was why these past few months had been so hard for him. In his normal world, he and Alice would've been doing this that first night, drunk with the taste of tequila on their lips. But he'd been fighting it, fighting her, for all the good reasons. Reasons his mother would've been proud of.

But he'd lost, hadn't he? And he wasn't proud of himself. But at what point did you just say screw it, and throw yourself over the biggest, baddest bull in the chute? That's how Jake was accustomed to living his life, so tonight wasn't really that much of a shocker. What *was* a shocker, was that he'd managed to be a pretty good guy up to this point. He'd put Alice first, or had tried to. And this, right here, this giving in to everything he'd hungered for, would end up taking a piece of her with him. Maybe she didn't realize that yet, but he did. And his heart beat painfully, guiltily, as he lowered her down on the bed with the little chocolates on the pillows.

He swallowed hard as she gazed up at him. So trusting. So full of love. *Love.* Just like those thoughts of Becky's baby, he hadn't let himself go there, either. Jake didn't fall in love. Jake fell in lust. And then turned on Sports Center after. Yet, here he was. Staring back at her, and thinking things he wouldn't have believed a few weeks ago.

He took hold of her shirt and pulled it slowly over her

head. The light slipping in through the curtains bathed her skin in its silver glow. Her stomach was smooth and flat as river rock, her breasts swelling over her simple, white bra, pale as powder.

Lying there, she reached up and touched his abdomen as he straddled her with his lungs barely able to expand any more. He wondered if this was what it felt like to slip away. To let your body and heart give in to something bigger than you. He pushed back against the feeling, like he was used to pushing back against everything in his life. But he knew he wouldn't be able to do this much longer. Something would have to give. Or someone would have to walk away.

He lowered himself on top of her, and she wrapped her legs around the backs of his thighs. She was so warm, he imagined waves of heat rolling off her skin like fire. She cupped his face in her hands, pulling his head down to kiss her. If she was nervous, if she was scared, she wasn't letting on. He was glad. He needed her to want this as much as he wanted it. But at the moment, he didn't know how that was possible. He was so consumed with her, he couldn't think straight.

He kissed her jaw, her throat, the swell of her breasts. She arched her back underneath him, and mumbled something he couldn't hear.

Breathing hard, like a man on the edge, he turned toward her face in the moonlight.

"What?" he said, his voice low and ragged.

"I love—"

And before she could say it again, before she could regret it, he pressed his lips to hers.

Chapter Seventeen

ALICE SAT IN the breakfast nook of the old house with her hands wrapped around a mug of hot coffee. It was raining out. Had been raining for the last three days, and the chill of fall was in the air. She wore her most comfortable cardigan, oversized and soft as a lamb's ear. Perfect for nursing her current mood.

Licking her lips, she watched the raindrops make their way down the foggy glass. Beyond that, the maples in the yard shivered in the wind. Their leaves had gone from emerald green, to a touch of gold around the edges practically overnight. September was almost gone. And the thought of that was enough to make her throat ache all over again.

She rubbed her thumbs over the rim of the chipped mug. It was hard not to think about Jake. He still occupied nearly every corner of her brain, every nook and cranny of her poor, battered heart. But as bad as it felt now, those first few weeks after their trip to Chicago had been the worst. There'd even been a few days where she hadn't wanted to get out of bed, and if it hadn't been for her dad and Dana, she probably wouldn't have. But slowly, as time wore on, she'd found a new normal. She'd learned to live with the constant ache, and to push thoughts of him to the back of her mind where they couldn't torment her when she was supposed to be working, and trying to ease the pain of others.

But on days like today, she let her pain come. She opened her heart to it. She let it wash over her like a wave, because with it came the sweet memory of him. Of being underneath him in those tangled sheets, and of being wrapped in his arms until morning. As hard as it was to remember, she didn't want to forget. She'd loved him then. She loved him still. She would probably always love Jake Elliott, for better or worse.

"Well, I think I'm ready. If I'm not forgetting anything."

Alice startled at the sound of Dana's voice behind her. She turned to see her friend standing there with a rolling suitcase and an army green duffel bag slung over her shoulder.

"You look…" Alice pushed the coffee mug away and stood, clutching her chest. "You look…"

"What?" Dana asked, glancing down at her outfit. "You don't like it?"

"No, I do. You look beautiful."

Dana looked like Dana. Piercings and all. She wore a pair of black jeans with holes in the knees, a clunky pair of combat boots, and a blue flannel shirt. She was lovely, and she was going home to visit her father, without masking who she was in the least.

Her eyes filling with tears, Alice stepped forward and put her arms around her friend.

Dana laughed softly. "I decided if I was gonna go back,

he was going to have to accept me for me. This is me."

"Yes, it is. And you're perfect."

Alice pushed away and wiped her tears, embarrassed that she'd started crying. But to be fair, she cried a lot these days. The other night she'd burst into tears during a cat food commercial. It was what it was.

"You don't have to pretend with me," Dana said. "I know you, Alice. Remember?"

Alice sniffed. "What?"

"I know why you're crying, and it's not because I decided to go home."

"That's not true. These are tears of joy. I'm happy for you."

Dana watched her skeptically.

"Are you nervous?" Alice asked, ready to change the subject. This was Dana's day. It was a special moment, and she didn't want to go raining on her parade by being a snotty, teary mess.

"Yes. No... A little."

"It's okay. That's normal. This is a big deal, you know. You're a rock star, Dana. It takes a lot of guts doing what you're doing."

Dana worried her bottom lip with her teeth, making the piercing there sparkle. "I don't feel like a rock star. I feel..."

"What?"

"I don't know. A little scared, I guess."

"But you're doing it anyway."

The younger woman nodded. It felt like a million years since she'd cried in Alice's arms the day of Mr. Lopez's funeral. The day she'd said her father was ashamed of her. But it had only been a few months. And Dana had done a lot of soul searching since then, a lot of growing up. She knew that to find peace with her dad, she also had to find forgiveness. Alice realized this was a significant step in Dana's acceptance of herself, too. Because even though she seemed fearless to the outside world, she'd been a lost girl for a while. Just trying to find her way.

"I'm proud of you, kiddo. I wish I could be more like you."

Dana stared at her. "You're kidding, right? Look what you did this summer."

Alice gave her a small smile. It was hard to talk about this, but Dana understood. "You mean look *who* I did this summer."

"Damn straight. That took guts, too. It was scary to open yourself up to Jake, but you did it. You got to experience it. You got to experience him. And that was brave."

"Yeah. So brave that I can't go eight full hours without sobbing."

"Your heart is broken. You're allowed."

Alice nodded. "I guess. But I thought I'd be better by now. I thought I'd be more over him."

"I understand why you broke up. I do. It makes sense to me, and I'm usually the one telling you to be crazier. But maybe it's so hard because you didn't give yourself any real closure with him. You didn't let yourself say goodbye."

Alice wondered if there was some truth to that. But at the time, it had been a simple choice. She had to leave him before he left her. Sometimes she wondered if not calling him back had been the right thing to do. But then she remembered she'd ultimately given him a gift, had made it easier on both of them in the long run.

He'd been a gentleman after Chicago, but he hadn't planned on sticking around, and eventually, the handful of phone calls had drifted away to nothing at all. He hadn't pushed that hard, because there was nothing to push for. And that was okay. It was. She'd known that going in. Staying friends after the sex was a nice theory, but they'd both known the reality. And it was a price they'd been willing to pay.

"You never really got a chance to say goodbye to your mom, either," Dana added softly. "Did you?"

The rain pattered on the roof, and the grandfather clock ticked the seconds off faithfully from the other room. Alice's heart slowed in her chest, as the realization of this sunk in.

"No, she didn't."

They both turned at the sound of her dad's voice. He stood there in the doorway, his bushy white brows furrowed.

"I never told you your mom was sick, until she got really sick," he said. "And by then, you didn't get a chance to come to terms with it. We just wanted to protect you, honey. And now all you want to do is protect yourself. That's why you never called Jake back. Isn't it?"

Alice swallowed hard. There was no point in denying it. It all made perfect sense, fell in place like a psychological jigsaw puzzle. Her issues went back to her childhood. Like Jake's. Like Dana's. Like most people's. The trick was, not to let them dictate the rest of her life. But that was easier said than done.

"It doesn't matter, Dad. He wasn't going to stay anyway. He knew it. And so did I."

They were quiet then, all three, as the rain continued coming down against the windows. The house was cold, and Alice wrapped her arms around herself. The pain would ease. It might never vanish completely, but it would ease—she knew that. She just had to lean into it. Learn from it. And move on.

Alice's dad touched Dana's elbow. "We'd better get going if we want to get you to the airport in time."

Dana nodded, looked at Alice one more time with a tenderness that touched her to the core, then headed to the front door, rolling the suitcase behind her.

"Text me!" she called after her.

Alice's dad stood there, working the car keys in his hand. He wasn't usually a man of few words, always opting to overshare, than share nothing at all. But she could tell he was struggling with something.

She stepped forward. "What is it, Dad?"

He sighed, looking older than he had in a while. "What Dana said makes a lot of sense. Closure…it's important. Being able to say your piece, or at least feel what you need to feel, is important. And maybe he needs that too, honey."

Alice watched him. She'd never thought about it that way. She'd always just assumed Jake wasn't hurting. At least not as much as she was. But what if, deep down, he had a wound that needed salve, too? What if showing him that she loved him, but didn't expect anything in return, eased an ache for him? Wasn't that the kind of thing you did for people you cared about?

"I don't really know this boy," her dad said. "But he's human, I know that much. And to have you in his life, and then to have you walk out of it...well. That's got to be tough. Even for the toughest cowboy."

He smiled at her. And with her eyes stinging, she smiled back. She watched him walk out of the breakfast nook with his keys in his hand. He was limping a little today. Maybe too much golf this last weekend. Or maybe too much work for a man well past retirement age. Whatever the reason, the image coaxed fresh tears from her eyes. He was a good man. The best. And his advice had always allowed her to negotiate some of life's steepest hills.

Sniffing, she wiped her cheeks. She'd go see Jake ride. That would convey something that words never could, no matter how hard she'd tried.

And she'd wear her green dress.

JAKE LEANED AGAINST an old, splintered gatepost, and watched as the flag team galloped their horses like bats out of hell around the arena, their flags from various sponsors waving chaotically behind them. The crowd loved this part. It got everyone pumped up for the rodeo, as country music blasted over the loudspeakers. Today, it was *Flatliner* by Cole Swindell. Even Jake's heartbeat had kicked up a notch, but that probably had more to do with being back in the arena for the first time since his shoulder had taken a dump on him. Whatever the reason, he was on edge, his stomach feeling tight and quivery, along with every muscle in his body.

He looked around. The stands were packed. The Copper Mountain Rodeo always brought in a good crowd, but today was especially perfect, with the sun coming out for the first time in days, and the temperature rising into the sixties—a rarity for this late in September.

The sharp smell of sawdust and animals filled his senses. The sound of the music, of the crowd cheering, of hooves thundering over the arena floor, made him anticipate what was coming. He'd drawn a bull named Tequila Sunrise, who was small and wiry, and who had a habit of spinning like an absolute thing of beauty. But it was his name that Jake kept coming back to. Even now as he stretched his arm over his chest like EJ had taught him, and felt the muscles and tendons there pull with a distinct tightness.

Tequila... Tequila, or more specifically tequila shots, and the night at the Wolf Den kept trying to work their way past his frontal lobe. But out of a need for pure survival, Jake had pushed it to the furthest, darkest corners of his mind these last few weeks. He hadn't allowed himself to think about Alice, to wonder what she was doing, or who she might be doing it with. And when he had gone there in a moment of weakness, he'd climbed onto his motorcycle and headed to the fairgrounds, a place where he'd always felt the most in control, to scrub his mind clean of her. So there were only thoughts of rodeo, of getting back into the game, and the money, where he belonged.

Still, his heart had a way of betraying him. At the weirdest times, when he should've been one hundred percent invested in climbing on the back of a bull and thinking only of staying the hell on. But she always came back to him. Her face, her scent, the way she'd felt in his arms just that once. But it'd only taken one time to show him a glimpse of a life he didn't feel like he deserved, or that he'd be any good at. What if he failed? What if he failed her? In the end, the night they'd slept together had been a fork in Jake's country road—embark on a journey he wasn't altogether sure he'd finish, or take the easy route, the route that was tried and true, and had never caused him any heartache. Not once.

So, here he was. A coward in the simplest terms. He pulled his Stetson low over his eyes and rolled his head from one shoulder to the other. It didn't matter. He was back on the circuit. And hell, maybe it wouldn't last much longer, but wasn't that what he'd told himself he'd wanted? To rodeo until he couldn't anymore? And he'd continue telling himself that, right along with the fact that he didn't need Alice. He didn't need anyone.

One of his buddies walked past and slapped him on the back. "Good to have you back, man. How's the shoulder?"

Jake nodded. "Good as new."

The announcer finished listing the sponsors on the loudspeaker, then breathed heavily into the mic. "Who's ready for some rooodeooo?"

The crowd went nuts.

"Welcome to Copper Mountain Rodeo, folks, where these cowboys and cowgirls are ready to give you a great show! Let's show them some Montana *love*!"

The crowd went apeshit. Popcorn flew. Little kids were hoisted onto their parents' shoulders. The flag team's sweaty horses stood quivering and stomping their hooves, sending dust into the air. Jake loved it. Loved every second. But there were things he was beginning to love more. No matter how hard he fought against them.

He screwed his eyes shut for a second, clearing his head. Listening to the sound of the rodeo. Feeling his chaps squeeze his thighs, and his paper number hanging on the back of his shirt. He was hyper aware of it. All of it. And when he opened his eyes again, he looked back into the stands where half of the crowd was on its feet to see the first barrel racer explode into the arena on a big chestnut gelding. It wasn't until right that second that he realized he was hoping to see her there. In the crowd, looking back.

He swallowed hard and ran his tongue over his lips. And what the hell would that change? It'd change nothing. Not a damn thing. She'd still be afraid of losing him to rodeo. And he'd still be afraid of losing himself to her.

He turned away. Toward the chutes and the bulls, and Tequila Sunrise standing still as a bronze statue in the sun.

Right before a flash of green might've caught his eye.

Chapter Eighteen

"EXCUSE ME. PARDON me. So sorry…" Alice stepped as carefully as she could between people, over cowboy boots, and away from sticky blobs of cotton candy on the floor of the stands. She'd never been to a rodeo before. But the atmosphere reminded her of the White Sox game—the smell of the popcorn and the energy of the crowd brought it all back. Brought him back to her, and she let him come. That's what she was here for, after all. To help them both heal. If she could find a seat before he actually started riding.

The thought of seeing him on the back of a bull made her stomach clench. But not nearly as much as the next thought that wanted to barge its way in—the image of him on the ground being gored or trampled. The image of him being taken away from her for good.

"Miss, there's a seat over here!"

She looked up to see an elderly woman in a hot pink cowboy hat waving her over. She smiled gratefully and stepped around a few more people who were trying to see around her.

"Oh, thanks so much," she said, sitting down on the other side of her, right next to the edge of the stands. It was the very front row, something she'd been hoping for, but hadn't expected to find once she saw the enormity of the crowd walking in. "I bought my ticket late. I didn't realize there'd be such a long line."

"There's *always* a line. Is this your first rodeo?" The woman smiled, dozens of wrinkles deepening all over her face, and chuckled at her own joke.

"Actually, it is."

"Well, you're in for a treat then, hon. It's a good time."

Alice smiled and set her purse down beside her on the bench. It was dirty, probably bursting with all kinds of fun germs, but for the first time ever, she really didn't care. *Huh.* Go figure.

"Are you here to see Misty Cummings ride?" the woman asked, sipping her drink from a red Solo cup, her turquoise rings catching the light. "She's from Billings. Been setting all kinds of records since last fall."

"Oh…no, actually. I'm just here for everything. The whole kit and caboodle." *Kit and caboodle?* She smiled at the woman, feeling awkward. In her green dress, she was probably sticking out like a sore thumb. But she couldn't help it. She was a romantic. And to her, the dress was where it had all started. Where she'd danced with Jake, and felt his arms around her for the first time. It was like her prom dress, and her cheeks heated as she looked down and smoothed the delicate material.

"Uh-huh." The older woman nodded slowly, looking her up and down, missing roughly nothing. Alice did not look like a woman who was here for the whole kit and caboodle.

Alice looked like a woman who was here for the caboodle, and the caboodle only. "Well, you got here just in time then. Popcorn?"

"Oh. Thank you." Alice took a handful, hesitated for a moment before putting it in her mouth, because, let's face it, she was better, but not cured. And then ate every kernel. It was so good, so warm and salty and buttery, that she couldn't even let herself wonder where this nice lady's hands had been. "That's so good."

"Can't have rodeo without the popcorn. Well, I guess you could. But I wouldn't want to."

The crowd stomped and cheered around them, as a rodeo clown began dancing to *Kick The Dust Up* by Luke Bryan, one of Alice's favorite songs. It made her think of the country, and parties, and beer, and hot summer nights. Things she'd never experienced before all at once, but had secretly wanted to.

Now, here she was. Among the countriest of country people. For someone born and raised in Montana, it had taken her long enough.

The clown danced some more, feigning hurt feelings when the announcer told him to make way for the next barrel racer. He turned toward the booth where the announcer sat, kissed his hand, and slapped it against his overall-clad rear end. The crowd laughed, and the announcer cracked a joke, as another thumpy country song began playing over the speakers. And then, like a bolt of lightning, a jet-black horse exploded into the arena, its rider leaning forward, with her hair flying behind her. Alice watched in wonder as the woman and horse moved as one, thundering around the barrels, one, two, three, and then galloped home, dirt flying, past the crowd that was on its feet.

"Sixteen point two seconds, folks! Let's hear it for Carly Rae Johnson all the way from Willows, California! Let's give her a nice Marietta welcome, shall we?"

The stands obliged, and the young woman on the dancing black horse smiled and waved from the other side of the arena.

Alice took a deep breath and finally let her gaze settle to her right, where a small herd of bulls stood in a round paddock. They were huge animals. Some with horns, some without, but they all looked capable of murder. In front of the paddock were chutes, and that's where the cowboys were. Some leaned on the fence watching the crowd, some were talking to their buddies, or just looking quiet, lost in thought.

With her heart in her throat, Alice studied each and every one. Watching for Jake's trademark white Stetson, his thick shoulders, his distinctive, sexy stance. And then, suddenly, there he was. Tall, gorgeous, tan. And looking right at her.

All of a sudden, she couldn't breathe. Her heart hammered behind her breastbone like it was trying to find a way out. Why in the world had she thought this was a good idea? She was breaking all over again. She'd leave here in pieces, which was exactly what she'd been trying to avoid.

He stood there, still as the gatepost he leaned against. He looked different today. He wore a hat she hadn't seen before—this one was darker, the color of chocolate. And it looked good on him, complimented his smooth, bronzed skin. His denim shirt was open at the throat, and his big, silver belt buckle glinted in the sun. He was in his element. Here, in the arena, with the bulls moving behind him, he looked fearless, ready to take on the world.

He looked up into the stands. And then, he smiled. So slowly, that her knees went weak.

The woman beside her let out a soft sound and nudged Alice in the side. "I see why you came out today."

Alice had no idea what to say. There was no use arguing. It was probably written all over her face, anyway.

"He's a handsome devil," the woman said. "A tall drink of water, like my mama used to say."

"And he knows it, too."

"They all know it, hon."

Another barrel racer, the last one apparently, galloped into the arena and tore around the barrels in a blur. The crowd went wild, but Alice couldn't take her eyes off Jake. They watched each other for another pregnant moment, before he reached up and tipped his hat at her. A simple, old-fashioned gesture, and one that made her want to melt into a puddle where she sat.

"Are you ready?" the woman asked her, taking another sip of her drink. "It's about time for the bull riding."

As if on cue, the clown came dancing out into the now empty arena, and began clapping to the music. The energy pulsing through the crowd was almost palpable. Alice didn't know much about rodeo, but she did know that the bull riding was the big draw. The main event. Her stomach dropped like it was tied to a cinderblock.

She watched Jake turn toward the chutes. She felt like she was going to throw up. Legitimately. All over the nice woman beside her who'd shared her popcorn. She couldn't even appreciate how amazing his butt looked in those chaps, because she was so preoccupied with not passing out. *Please keep him safe, God. Please don't let him get hurt...*

Wringing her hands in her lap, she kept her gaze firmly on Jake. This was it. Her worst fear. Being in the crowd watching this craziness unfold. But now that she was here, she wouldn't look away. No matter how sick she felt. No matter how scared. It was why she'd come. To show him she was here for it. At least this one time.

"Folks!" the announcer yelled over the mic. "Who's ready for some *bull riding*?"

The people in the stands cupped their hands over their mouths and yelled back. Some stood, stomping their boots on the floorboards. The sound was almost deafening.

The cowboys near the chutes rolled their heads from side to side. The bulls in the pen snorted and pawed at the ground. The place was electric, pulsing. It was all Alice could do to sit still.

As if reading her mind, the lady beside her patted her knee. "It'll be all right, hon. They know what they're doing."

Alice forced a smile.

A cowboy in a blue plaid shirt climbed up on the chute, where inside, a large, brown bull stood. Several other cowboys held it, tugging on the thick strap around its girth, as the cowboy in plaid put his leg over the animal with surprising grace.

"Folks, this cowboy right here is from Tempe, Arizona," the announcer cooed into the mic. "All the way from Tempe, to the Copper Mountain Rodeo. Let's hope it was worth the trip!"

Alice took a steadying breath as she craned her neck and looked for Jake. She couldn't see him anymore. But he was down there, somewhere among the animals and men. Ready to put on a show for these people who idolized him, but really didn't know him from Adam. Alice's heart ached for the guy in the bookstore that day. The one who'd read Stephen King as a boy. The one who'd kissed her next to the bookmark display. It wasn't that he was any better than the Jake in the arena now. But he was a safer bet than this Jake. Someone she could assume might be around next year. Or next month. Or tomorrow.

The crowd held its collective breath as the bull stood still in the chute for a few short seconds. And then the gate exploded outward.

The animal threw itself into the arena in a mass of muscle and ropy saliva. The cowboy held on with one hand, the other waving over his head like he was grabbing for some stars.

Alice watched through eyes that felt as wide as dinner plates. This was Jake's job. This was what he did from nine to five. Holding on for dear life. Trying not to get thrown into Canada somewhere. And liking it.

The bull twisted and kicked, sending his hind legs

punching into the air. It seemed like hours before it finally succeeded in throwing the cowboy off. Not into Canada, but far enough that the poor guy had definitely experienced the wonder of flight. And it hadn't taken hours. It had only taken five point two seconds.

The cowboy from Tempe jumped up and darted away from the bull who was charging straight for him. The crowd gasped as the rodeo clown waved his arms in a brave attempt at distraction. It worked. The bull peeled away at the last second, and the stands erupted in relieved applause.

Alice took enough of a breath to satisfy her lungs, and looked around. Everyone was glued to the arena. And she understood in that moment one of the reasons why Jake must love this so much. It would be a powerful thing to have people think you were invincible. Might even help you believe it yourself.

"Folks!" the announced yelled over the speakers. "Let's give this cowboy some Montana love!"

The crowd cheered even louder, and the cowboy took off his hat and waved it in the air.

"Our next young man needs no introduction, but we'll introduce him anyway! Put those hands together for Marietta's own Jake Elliott!"

The people in the stands jumped to their feet, whistling and calling his name.

She watched Jake lean over the chute, waiting for the big red bull inside to calm some. The animal rammed itself against the gate, and several cowboys leaned down, trying to get him in a good enough position for Jake to climb on.

Alice's heart was beating so fast, it felt more like a steady hum. Her palms were damp, her knees shaking. She watched and prayed, and that became a steady hum, too. *Keep him safe, keep him safe...*

The woman sitting beside her patted her leg. "It'll be all right, hon."

She nodded, but had to pull her bottom lip between her teeth to keep it from trembling. Despite everything, despite knowing Jake was a PBR champion, and was really, really good at this, she couldn't shake the feeling of dread in her lower belly.

And then, when she looked back at the chutes, he was already astride the bull—the wild, red animal with the lopped-off horns. A hush fell over the crowd. One second. Two... Jake lowered his head, his cowboy hat concealing his face, and punched his hand holding the strap.

Alice stopped breathing. Her heart slowed in her chest. And then he gave a quick nod. And the gate shot open.

At that moment, she was only aware of three things—her own breathing echoing in her ears. Her shaking hands clutching her chest. And the image of Jake on the thrashing bull, swimming in front of her eyes. Time had slowed to a steady drip, the seconds stretching into hours. And still the bull bucked. Twisted. And then turned into a spin.

Jake clung to his back, his long legs wrapped around the animal like they were meant to be. His arm was raised over his head, and he looked as graceful as a dancer right then. Alice had no idea when she'd started crying. But tears streamed down her face, dripping warmly onto her hands.

"Eight seconds and *still* going, folks!"

The announcer's voice was barely audible over the screaming of the crowd. This was what they'd come for. To see a hero renew their faith in the American West. Alice could feel it, coursing through her own veins. It had been beyond her before. *This* had been beyond her. But not today. Today, she felt the magic. If only for a little over eight seconds.

And then, suddenly, the bull came to a stop. Dirt and dust rose around it in a cloud. Jake sat there, his body stiff with anticipation. Then, without any warning, the animal shot straight into the air.

The crowd gasped. A sound escaped Alice's throat— something between a squeak and a moan. She leaned forward, straining to see between the metal railings separating the stands from the arena.

The bull came down hard. Jake's body jolted violently. His head hit the animal's massive withers with a smack. And then he was out. He collapsed like a rag doll and slid lifelessly off the side.

Alice stood and cried out. The sound of the crowd died to a low drone in her ears. There was only Jake. And the image of him being dragged now, his hand still caught up in the strap. The bull being distracted by one clown, while another one rushed in to work him free.

She was vaguely aware she was still crying. But out of terror now. Her worst nightmare coming true. *Jake...* His name was on her lips, in her heart. Always in her heart. What if she'd done this? What if she'd brought all her neurosis and negative energy into this place, and they'd attached themselves to him somehow? She'd heard of weirder things. How could she have thought being here would be any kind of help to him? Any kind of strength?

She struggled to take a full breath as the rodeo clown spun in the same direction as the bull, staying with Jake, pulling at his arm, until finally, it was loose.

He crumpled in the dirt like something lifeless. The woman beside her had stood, too. Her arm was around Alice, helping her stay upright.

"Can I go down there?" Alice panted, half to herself.

"No, no, honey. You stay right here. They'll help him out, but you have to steer clear."

Two cowboys on horseback flanked the bull, and drove him back toward the chute. Several men and women rushed out and knelt beside Jake who wasn't moving. The announcer said something to the crowd, which was silent now, but Alice couldn't comprehend the words. Off to the side, she could see an ambulance, its lights on, its motor running. It had been staged near the entrance to the arena, but she hadn't noticed until now. *Oh, God, oh God...*

"Ladies and gentleman, we're being told Jake is awake..."

Alice waited, the world moving in slow motion around her.

"But he's gonna head over to the hospital to get checked out."

She blinked. Then let out a long, shaky breath.

"Give this fella a nice round of applause, all right? He's

your champion tonight, with the longest ride so far! He's going to be a tough act to follow."

The crowd clapped and cheered, but it was a more subdued version of its former self. The comforting words of the announcer weren't doing much to persuade everyone, since he still wasn't moving as the EMTs ran toward him with a stretcher.

Alice was vaguely aware that the older woman still had an arm around her. She was grateful. She leaned into the soft warmth, as tears rolled down her cheeks.

"He'll be okay, hon," the woman said.

Picking up her purse, Alice turned. "Thank you. I don't know what I would've done if you hadn't been here."

"Oh, you would've been just fine."

"I'm going to go follow the ambulance," she said. "But I'm Alice, by the way. Alice Bloom."

"Betty Frank. Nice to meet you, Alice."

And just like that, Alice had made a new friend. She had Jake to thank for that. She had Jake to thank for so many things.

But as she walked carefully down the steps leading away from the stands, she knew it wouldn't be enough to truly change her heart. The pain of seeing Jake hurt was too much to bear. The thought of losing him, unthinkable. The instinct to protect herself was so strong, she trembled from it. Or maybe that was just her old friend, fear. She'd stood up to it more in these last few months than she ever had before. But tonight, it was going to have the last word. Tonight, she'd cut him free for good.

It was the only way.

Chapter Nineteen

"YOU'RE LUCKY, YOU know," EJ was saying. "The way you were hanging, that bull should've ripped your arm clean off."

Jake stretched his legs in the emergency room bed. It was too short for him, and his boots were hanging off the side. A small price to pay. His physical therapist was right. He was lucky. He'd had a lot of close calls on the circuit. But something about tonight felt different. Maybe it was the bump on his head. It throbbed like a son of a bitch.

"I know," he said, moving his arm over his chest and wiggling his fingers. "It doesn't even hurt that bad. Weird."

EJ was standing over him, hands in his slacks pockets. He'd just happened to be working in-patient at the hospital tonight, and had heard what happened as Jake was being brought in. Marietta couldn't keep a secret that way. But it was part of the charm of living in a small town. Other people knew you'd almost died before you did.

"We're going to have to wait a few days for the swelling to go down, but right now, I'd say the shoulder held up better than I expected. It's your head I'm most worried about."

Apparently, so were the ER docs. Jake was being admitted overnight for observation and a few tests. Routine, they'd said. But he'd still had to call his family and tell them not to come. There were so many of them. And honestly, he felt strange. Overwhelmed. Like a switch inside him had been flipped, and it was lighting up his insides in all different colors. He needed to process that. Plus, he'd be in one of those awesome backless hospital gowns, so there was that.

EJ was talking about tendons and trauma. Jake was only following some of it. He managed to nod at the appropriate times, and answer a few questions, but mostly he was going over and over the ride in his head. But that wasn't quite right—he was going over the minutes *before* the ride in his head. The minutes leading up to it, when he'd spotted Alice in the stands. In that green dress. The one that made her look like a dark-haired apparition. The one that made his heart betray his common sense, because he'd known they weren't going to work. Or, at least that's what he'd convinced himself of just a few minutes before.

But when he'd seen her there, knowing she was going against her grain and everything that made her tick as a woman, it had done something to him. That might actually have been the moment the switch flipped. Maybe it hadn't been the bump on his head at all. Because in that moment, he recognized more similarities between them than differences. They both loved each other. That was pretty obvious now. And with love, wasn't everything else supposed to fall into place if you'd let it?

The problem was, Jake wasn't accustomed to letting anything fall into place. He was accustomed to burying things. And if they wouldn't stay buried, he was used to fighting them until his hands bled. But this feeling? The one that had settled over him the second he'd opened his eyes on the arena floor... It wasn't something that was going to die easily. And maybe it wouldn't die at all. Maybe he was in for the fight of his life. Or the ride of his life. He wasn't quite sure yet.

"So, I heard you took the money tonight," EJ was saying. "Not surprised, since you stayed on long enough for the crowd to grab dinner and a movie."

Jake laughed. Then winced. His head hurt. "Yeah, it was a good night."

"Aside from the possible concussion."

"Aside from that."

"So, what do you do with all that prize money?" EJ asked, crossing his arms over his chest. "It's got to be piling up right about now."

Jake hadn't told anyone about Buckshot. About his kind of, sort of idea about *maybe* becoming a stock contractor in the future. But at that very moment, lying in the hospital bed, with only images of Alice in that green dress dancing behind his eyes, it didn't seem so odd saying it out loud. Like he wasn't giving up on something, but leaning into something else instead.

"I've been putting it away," Jake said evenly. "Thinking about buying a bull and getting into the stock contractor trade."

A slow smile spread over EJ's mouth. He'd never made

his opinions about the longevity of a bull-riding career any secret over the years. He looked like it was his birthday and Christmas all rolled into one.

"Will you look at that," he said, shaking his head. "You finally came around."

"I said I was thinking about it. Never said I was doing it, Dad."

But it was too late. EJ was thrilled. And Jake couldn't even be annoyed. It felt surprisingly good to confide in someone. Seeing on their face what they thought of the idea. And if his friend's expression was any indication, Jake was on the right track.

"Knock, knock," came a soft voice on the other side of the curtain. "Jake?"

Jake froze. EJ looked at him, his brows raised. It sounded like Alice. But his head was still fuzzy, and there was a slight ringing in his ears, so he couldn't be sure.

He scooted himself up to a sitting position. "Yeah?"

After a second, the curtain whispered open, and she stepped in. *Alice.* In her green dress. Looking gorgeous. And scared to death.

She glanced at EJ and gave him a small smile. "I'm sorry. Am I interrupting? I just wanted to see…" She let her voice trail off as she looked back at Jake again. Her skin was alabaster white. Her chin quivered slightly as she took him in.

And all he wanted to do was hold her. The urge was so strong, his arms ached from it. He cursed these last few weeks, these last few hours, when all he'd wanted was to show up on the doorstep of that funeral home, and pull her into his arms. But he hadn't. Why hadn't he again? Like his head, the reasons were fuzzy now. They seemed less important and harder to grasp on to. All he could really focus on was the feeling unfolding inside his chest at that minute. The feeling of not wanting to let her go.

"I'll just see you later, okay, Jake?" EJ smiled at Alice. Then pushed quietly past the curtain, and let it fall back into place behind him.

Jake stared at her, sensing the delicacy of the moment. And he was crappy with delicate things.

"I—"

"I—"

They both started at the same time, then stopped. All of a sudden there was an awkwardness between them that was born of that delicacy. He knew it would be hard to negotiate this without screwing it up.

"Ladies first," he said.

She stepped forward, staring at the bump on his head. He hadn't seen it yet, but he didn't need stitches, so that was good.

"I was just going to say, I wanted to see you."

He nodded slowly. "See me...before riding? Or after?"

"Both." Chewing the inside of her cheek, she looked down at her dress for a second before going on. "This feels kind of ridiculous now. Wearing this to a rodeo. But I was trying to tell you something that I was having a hard time with. Since, you know. Since Chicago..."

He waited, watching her. Praying the doctor wouldn't

come back in before she could finish.

"I couldn't really say it in words," she continued. "That's why I never called you back. I didn't know how to say what I wanted to say."

He knew exactly what she meant. The dress, which was the same one she'd worn to the Wolf Den when they'd danced that night, had hit him straight in the heart. Like an arrow, or a bullet, it had left a burning hole in its wake. She'd wanted him to feel something. Likely the same thing she was feeling. It wouldn't solve anything. But at least he'd know. He understood what she'd been trying to say perfectly. No words needed.

He swallowed, letting the room go quiet again. She was so pretty. And she looked so sad.

"You came tonight," he finally said, his voice raspy. "Seeing you up there, and in that..." He let his gaze fall to the dress, how it hugged her curves in the sweetest way, before looking back up again. "I know how hard it was for you to come."

She nodded, tears filling her eyes. "Well, it wasn't anything compared to seeing you get hurt. I'm not going to lie, that part almost did me in."

"But you're here."

"I'm here. I had to make sure you were okay." She swiped at her tears with the backs of her knuckles. She was breaking his heart.

"I'm okay, Alice. I know it looked scary, but I'm fine."

"You're fine. But it could've been different. You could've been killed."

"But I wasn't."

"But you could've been."

And this had been the line in the sand that very first night when they'd done the shots together. He'd been so adamant all this time, refusing to give an inch. Because giving in meant weakness. It meant needing her, wanting her, putting her above everything else, including rodeo. But tonight, that seemed like less of a weakness, than a logical next step in learning to love someone. He'd been so busy not letting himself need or want anything, that he'd managed to deny himself the very element of life that he'd been so sanctimonious about—the element of joyfully living in the moment.

All of this was still settling in his heart, in his mind, when she pulled in a breath to speak again. He almost stopped her. But she reached down and put her hand on his leg first. The weight of it was so light, it felt like a bird had landed there. And he was temporarily speechless.

"The truth is," she said, "that I'll always be a little afraid. Of everything. No matter how much I've learned since meeting you. I'm going to try and be better. Every day I'm going to try and be a little more adventurous. But there's a limit to what I can do, Jake. I'll never be able to be okay with this. With the kinds of risks you take. I'll never be okay with feeling the way I do tonight."

"So…you don't want to love me, because you might lose me."

She watched him. Then nodded slowly.

He knew arguing with that would be the most hypocritical thing ever, because, really, wasn't that exactly how he'd felt most of his life? He'd grown into the most callous man, always pushing things away that might affect him, good or bad. But he was tired of being callous. And he was tired of denying himself things that really mattered. Joy. Green-eyed women who loved him. Future babies with chubby cheeks and sticky fingers. A life at home, and not on the road in lonely hotel rooms and towns he couldn't remember the names of. Jake was just tired, period. And suddenly, tonight, he felt like an old man in a young man's body. Bruised and battered, and ready for some softness.

"It doesn't have to be that way, Alice."

She took a step back. He could hear familiar voices outside, footsteps coming closer. His doctor and a few nurses. Terrible timing. The absolute worst.

"It is what it is." She'd looked away, and was clutching her purse, her knuckles white. "But I didn't want to leave without saying goodbye. Without letting you know how I feel about you. And I'm so glad you're okay, Jake. My heart—"

The curtain slid open, and his doctor stood there, flanked by two nurses in purple scrubs. "Mr. Elliott," she said over her readers. "It's time for your CT scan."

Alice turned and bumped into one of the nurses. "Sorry," she mumbled, before looking over at Jake one more time. His chest felt like it was splitting wide open. Cracking, like the trunk of a tree after a lightning strike.

"Goodbye, Jake."

And then she was gone. Leaving the slightest trail of perfume in her wake.

He watched the space where she'd been, his mouth open slightly. The doctor was talking, but he didn't hear a word.

Chapter Twenty

JAKE PULLED UP to the curb in front of Bloom Funeral Home, his big truck rumbling through the crisp October air. The leaves had changed around town, in the mountains beyond. Mother Earth was having a party—red, orange, yellow confetti reigned supreme, and there was even a faint dusting of snow on top of Copper Mountain. The mild weather from the last days of September were just a memory now. Winter was right around the corner.

He cut the engine and sat there for a minute, looking over at the regal old house. He'd tried calling Alice since the rodeo, but she wouldn't answer. He'd come to see her, but she was never home. He refused to leave what he had to say on her damn voicemail, so he was now in unfamiliar territory. Chasing down a woman, who by all accounts, didn't seem to want to be caught.

Patting his shirt pocket for the second time that afternoon, he made sure the small envelope was still there. Then reached for the handle and opened the door.

It was quiet on the street today, a Sunday afternoon with a bright sun hanging low in the sky. Clouds were trying to gather in the distance, but didn't seem like they wanted to muster the effort. He took a deep breath, letting the autumn air saturate his lungs. Then set his jaw, and headed up the walkway to the door.

There was a light on in the sitting room—one of the old-fashioned lamps with a pink shade that gave the place such character. Didn't necessarily mean anyone was going to answer the door, but he planned on being a pain in the ass until they did.

Steeling himself, he raised his fist. But before he could knock, the door opened with a squeak.

Standing there, watching him through coal-black eyeliner, was Dana.

Jake stared back as a heaviness settled between them. She knew exactly why he was here, but had probably been told to turn him away. She probably also knew by the look on his face that he wasn't leaving without a fight.

"Hey, Dana," he said, his voice even.

"Hey, Jake."

He put his hands in his jeans pocket, looking as casual as he could manage. "Is Alice here?"

"Sorry, she's not."

Unconvinced, he looked over her shoulder to the entryway, expecting what, he didn't know. Alice, standing there looking back? But the place looked quiet, empty. Devoid of the light she brought to every room she walked into.

His gaze shifted back to the young woman in front of him, and she gave him a sad smile.

"I know you don't believe me," she said. "But I promise, she's not here this time."

This time. His stomach dropped. Even though he'd known she'd been avoiding him, that still stung. Jake wasn't used to having the door shut in his face. Or the door not opening for him at all. It was humbling. But if he'd learned anything these last few weeks, it was that he'd needed a good dose of humbling.

"Oh…" he said. Sounding more like a lovesick boy than a grown-ass man. His neck heated.

Dana's pretty face fell, and she stepped back. "Would you like to come in for a minute? It's chilly out there."

He smiled, nodded, and stepped in the entryway. The house smelled like coffee. It was warm inside, cozy. And he thought back to when he'd pulled up to the curb for Elaine's funeral, and he'd been creeped out by the old place. But now, he had a soft spot for its elderly, quirky vibe. He'd opened himself to it. Just another thing about him that had changed recently.

"Sometimes I come here on Sundays," Dana said, pulling her black sweater tighter around her shoulders. "It's peaceful. A great place to read, or just think."

She didn't have to explain. He understood. Even though he wasn't much of a reader, or hadn't been most of his adult life, he thought he could probably get back into it again with a place like this to inspire him. And the thinking thing…well. He'd done enough of that to last a lifetime.

"I get it," he said. "It's nice."

Dana watched him, narrowing her dark eyes. Maybe she was sizing him up. Maybe getting ready to tell him to get lost for good. He tried to think of a way to convince her how he felt about Alice. A way to get her to admit where she was.

Jesus. He just needed to put it all on the table. Why did he always have to make everything so complicated? It was as simple as a few damn words, anyway.

"I love her," he finally said. And waited as the revelation settled over them like a blanket.

Dana stood there for a minute, stoic. Or trying to be stoic, before her expression finally softened. "I know you do. I can tell."

He exhaled slowly, realizing he'd been holding his breath. It was the first time he'd said it out loud. It felt like he'd finally stopped struggling against the current, and was letting it carry him where it really wanted to go.

"When she came to the hospital that night," he said, "I should've told her. I should've told her then, but I didn't know how. And then I ran out of time. She left, and…" He shrugged, not knowing how to finish. *She broke my heart?* She *had* broken his heart when she'd walked out of that room, but he had nobody to blame but himself. He was the unknown variable in this equation, and he'd been pretty clear about that from the beginning. At the end of the day, he didn't know if it had anything to do with bull riding at all. Maybe she could've been with a bull rider all along, if he'd given enough of himself to make the ride worthwhile.

Whatever. None of that mattered now. What mattered now was finding her so he could tell her himself. And then, if she still wanted to walk away, he'd let her. But he wasn't going to let her go without saying what he needed to.

Dana worried her bottom lip with her teeth, looking like

she wanted to tell him something, but was wrestling with it.

"Jake?"

He turned the sound of the voice behind him. There, standing in the doorway, was Alice's dad. He smiled, and stepped forward to shake Jake's hand.

"Sir," he said. "Nice to see you again."

"Nice to see you too, son."

"I was just hoping to talk to Alice," Jake said. "But Dana said she's not home."

Dana and Charles exchanged looks. Jake didn't have to be a mind reader to know she'd sworn them to secrecy. He clenched his jaw, wanting to see her now more than ever. She was officially on the run. And if there was anything Jake understood, it was that.

He licked his lips, which felt dry as a bone. Then cleared his throat. But before he could ask where she was, Charles held up a hand.

"I know why you're here," the older man said. "But I should tell you, she made us promise not to interfere this time. She was adamant."

Dana frowned. "It's true. She made me pinkie swear, and that's pretty sacred."

Jake nodded. He put his hands in his pockets, and paused, trying to find the right words. Praying they wouldn't elude him. Because this moment could be a turning point, for him, for Alice. But they had to trust him with it first.

"I know she doesn't want to see me," he said quietly. "And I know why. She'd afraid of this. Afraid I'll screw it up." He shrugged, feeling the self-consciousness sink into his very bones. But he plowed forward anyway. "I was afraid I'd screw it up, too. For a long time, before I even met Alice, I'd been afraid of messing things up that were important to me. So I ended up avoiding anything too hard by closing myself off and telling myself I was too tough for it anyway. That's how I've lived my life up until now. Closed off. And I know Alice is afraid, too. But I think together, we might be able to help each other with the hard stuff. The things that scare us."

Charles and Dana watched him steadily. Dana's eyes had grown soft, misty. Charles's had a look of nostalgia in them that Jake recognized might be for someone in his past. Probably Alice's mother. He knew he'd lost her too soon. That he'd never remarried, choosing instead to put all his strength into raising their daughter alone. Charles Bloom had known love and loss better than Jake ever had.

"Alice has helped me with hard stuff, too," Dana said. "Things I was afraid of. And I'm here to tell you, tackling the hard stuff is worth it. I promise."

Charles stepped close, and put a fatherly arm around her shoulders. She had a lighter energy around her today than when he'd seen her last at Marietta Western Wear, and he wondered if Alice had anything to do with that. If she had, he wouldn't have been surprised. Alice had a certain energy around her, too.

Charles nodded, as if remembering something. Or deciding something. Then looked up at Jake, his blue eyes bright. "You're absolutely right. She's scared. But I don't think I realized until this very second that I'm more scared for her than she is for herself."

Jake stood still. Listening. Opening himself up to everything Charles Bloom had to say.

"She's turning her back on something right now," Charles murmured. "And that's not what her mom would've wanted for her. It sure isn't what I want for her. She'll never know true happiness if she can't…"

"I won't hurt your daughter, Mr. Bloom," Jake said. "You have my word on that."

Charles nodded again, weighing this.

His entire adult life, Jake had avoided quiet entryways with steely-eyed fathers who had no room in their hearts for bullshit or empty declarations of love. But for the first time ever, he thought he might understand what it would be like standing there in the other set of shoes. If Alice was his daughter, he'd want that promise, too. No matter how much he wanted her to spread her wings and fly.

"I'll hold you to it, Jake."

They watched each other for another few seconds, with what Jake felt like was a new and tender bargain between them. The grandfather clock ticked from the other room. Jake's heart beat steadily inside his chest. It was a moment he thought he might remember for the rest of his life.

Dana looked up at Charles hopefully. "I pinkie swore," she said. "But you didn't, Mr. Bloom."

Chapter Twenty-One

ALICE LOOKED AROUND one more time, making sure she was still alone. The temperature had dropped since she'd left the house, and goose bumps rose along her exposed skin.

Shivering, she looked up at the lovely canopy of evergreens overhead. A soft, but chilly breeze whispered through the pines, and was the only sound except for the calling of a flock of Canadian geese across the lake. Soon, its deep blue surface would be frozen over, and ice skaters would come from far and wide to etch figure eights into its frosty glass.

But today, the lake moved with the wind. Tiny waves made their way to the rocky shore, and washed over Alice's bare feet with little splashes. Hugging herself, she wiggled her toes and looked out toward Copper Mountain in the distance. Right then, it looked more purple than blue, the clouds galloping across the sky, mirroring its blackberry color. The sun would set soon, setting those very clouds on fire, and she wondered where she'd be then. Sitting in her robe and slippers in front of a warm fire? Or driving across town toward something that was as unknown and ever-changing as the pattern of those clouds themselves? She hadn't made up her mind yet. But she was working on it.

Brushing her hair away from her face, she stepped in the lake, feeling the muddy silt ooze between her toes. The water was so cold, it stole the breath from her lungs. Her teeth chattered, but she clamped her jaw shut and forced herself to take another step. The lake lapped around her ankles, and then her calves, pushing, pulling, making her sway on her feet.

She'd been thinking about this for days. Every time the phone rang, and she'd seen Jake's number on the screen, she thought about it. Every time she looked herself in the mirror, to face her reflection with the puffy eyes and chapped nose. And her eyes... She'd seen that look before. On so many people who'd walked through the doors of the funeral home over the years. Alice was in mourning. She was mourning Jake. But she was also mourning a part of herself that she'd never gotten around to setting free. The woman her mother would've been proud of. The one who wasn't afraid of her shadow, but turned to it instead, and asked it to dance.

She took another step, and the water lapped around her pale white thighs. She lowered her hands and touched her fingertips to the lake. Her nipples pebbled at the frigid air blowing against them, and she thought of Jake taking them into his mouth. How warm he'd been that night. How loving. And it gave her the courage to take another step.

She wondered if she ever would've found herself naked and stepping into Miracle Lake in October, if she'd never met Jake. She knew the answer to that. Since the night she'd first laid eyes on him, he'd been forcing her to take a closer look at herself. Was she living fully enough? Happily enough? Fearlessly enough? She'd known the answer to those questions, too. They'd been a resounding no. Before today. Today was a baptism. A challenge realized. A bet, won and lost.

Alice's teeth chattered as she took another step. Then another. The water lapped around her stomach now, and she had to remember to breathe as every muscle in her body stiffened painfully.

Nothing in her life was going to come with a guarantee. She knew that now. But more than knowing it, she was accepting it with every step deeper into the lake, which was alive with autumn and the promise of winter. She could get hypothermia from the cold. She could get attacked by a giant catfish, or some kind of fresh water shark. But she probably wasn't going to. She could die of a broken heart if she let herself fall the rest of the way in love with Jake, but she probably wasn't going to do that, either. Love was a part of life. So was pain. So was loss. And to experience the good, you had to be at peace with the possibility of the bad.

Taking another step, she pulled in a shaky breath, let her gaze settle on the golden horizon in the distance, and dipped herself under. Completely. With her whole heart.

The frigid water swirled in dark currents all around her. And then she broke the surface with a gasp. She pushed her hair away from her face. Then felt herself smile. She opened her eyes to the mountains, to the beautiful sky, to the lake, which she'd just given herself up to, and she laughed. It was the sound of being set free. She'd done it. She'd really done it…

"I'll be damned," said a low voice behind her.

She spun around with a yelp. Her arms flew to her breasts, covering them, even though the water was doing most of that for her.

Standing there on the shore, wearing a red plaid shirt and Wranglers that fit just right, was Jake. He had his hands on his hips, his head cocked to the side. A devilish smile on his handsome face.

"You're skinny-dipping, Bloom."

Her mouth fell open as water dripped into her eyes. She swiped it away with trembling hands. "What are you d-d-doing here?"

"Watching you lose our bet. And it might be the most beautiful thing I've ever seen."

Her heart was pounding from the shock, her pulse skipping wildly behind her ears.

"Come here, darlin'," he said, hooking his finger at her. "You're gonna freeze to death."

Still having a hard time believing he was actually there, she pushed through the freezing water and stepped toward him. Toward his warmth and vitality. Toward his unpredictability, and she realized that she'd always been walking toward Jake, in one way or another. He was her true north. And it didn't matter if he rode bulls for a living, or if he was an accountant safe behind a cubicle somewhere, she loved him. And that meant loving all of him.

She'd known it before, known it for weeks, maybe. But she smiled as the knowledge settled into her very being.

There was freedom in giving yourself up to the world. To its hectic spinning and chaotic tilt. She'd just have to wear a seat belt from here on out.

Looking him in the eyes, she stepped out of the water, exposing herself to the cold breeze, to his hungry gaze. She hugged herself, as if that would do any good. Her breasts swelled over her forearms as the water streamed from her hair down her shoulders. She watched with clicking teeth as he unbuttoned his shirt and peeled it off.

She stepped carefully onto the shore, the small rocks biting into the soles of her feet. And then, he pulled her into his arms, wrapping her in his shirt, which carried his warmth, his scent in its very fibers.

Resting her head on his bare chest, she closed her eyes and breathed him in. He held her so close, she could feel his heart thumping against her cheek, could hear its even cadence.

"My d-d-dad told you, didn't he?"

"You can't be mad," he said softly. "He didn't pinkie swear."

She laughed.

"You're so cold. Didn't you bring a towel?"

She shook her head. "I wasn't planning on g-g-getting in. I was only thinking about it."

"What sealed the deal?"

She pulled away enough to look up into his face. He was looking back with such tenderness, she knew something had changed between them. She wasn't sure yet if the skinny-dipping was a tipping point, but it had to have been a factor.

"You," she said.

He watched her. "Me…"

"I wanted to prove to myself that I could do it. And if I could do this, if I could do something this wild…and I mean, let's face it. For me this is wild."

He grinned.

"Then I could take you on too," she continued.

He wrapped the shirt tighter around her. It practically came to her knees, which was convenient. Since she was naked. And sopping wet. And happier than she'd ever been in her life.

"I like the sound of that," Jake said, his mouth moving against her temple. "I'm going to have to replace the adrenaline rush from rodeo. Can't think of a better way to do it than that."

She grew still. Her heart was beating right alongside his. They'd fallen in sync with each other. Just like that.

She pushed away and looked up at him again, her mouth open. "Jake—"

He put a finger to her lips, and the playful expression he always wore fell away then. And in that moment, she thought she saw him for who he really was. Not the balls-to-the-wall bull rider who'd stolen her heart. But the cowboy who was tucking it safely inside his pocket.

"This is a step I've been meaning to take for a while, darlin'," he said. "Seeing you in those stands…hell, seeing you *here.*" He paused, swallowing visibly. "Well, you inspire me. More than that, I guess. You give me the guts to go new places."

She smiled, her eyes blurry. "I didn't think you were scared of anything."

"I was scared of losing this bet."

"You won."

He brushed his knuckles across her cheeks. "And so did you."

She watched as he looked down and tapped the pocket of his shirt that was wrapped around her shoulders.

Putting her hand over it, she felt something there. Then pulled the pocket open enough to see an envelope inside.

"Open it," he said.

She took it out and held it for a minute, looking up at him questioningly.

"Go on..."

She waited another second, and then tore the paper open with trembling fingers. She'd almost forgotten she was supposed to be cold. Probably because with Jake, she kept smoldering from the inside out.

Inside, were two tickets. She pulled them out and stared at them in her hand.

Jake grinned. Like a teenager. "They're for *La Bohème*," he said. "It's playing at the Chicago Opera Theater right before Christmas. Hope you have a nice dress."

She grinned back, feeling her heart expand to fill up places inside her that had been empty until now. Feeling lighter than air, like she might float away, up into the candy-colored clouds at any second.

But Jake just put his arms around her again. Holding her close. Anchoring her in place. Where she'd always longed to be.

The crisp Montana breeze blew against her skin, moved through the pines above. Whispered in her ears, telling her a story as old as time. It started with a once upon a time, and ended with a happily ever after. It was their story. And it was only just beginning.

"I have just the dress," she said.

And kissed him long and deep.

Epilogue

THE TWIN ENGINES of the Cessna whirred through the winter afternoon, snow falling gently outside the windows onto the tarmac. Alice stopped short of pressing her nose into the foggy glass, and squinted at the control tower in the distance.

"Nervous?"

She turned to the handsome man sitting beside her. He smiled, managing to devastate her all over again. He wore a black jacket over the most gorgeous dark blue suit she thought she'd ever seen. His pinstripe tie was pale against his tanned skin, and was a perfectly delicious contradiction. The rough and tumble bull rider in a *GQ* suit.

"I'm okay," she said, smiling back. "Better than last time. We're not going to skid off the runway, are we?"

He reached over and grabbed her hand, tucking it firmly in his. Something that never failed to give her butterflies. It was just one of the things she loved about Jake. Add that to the list that kept growing by the day.

"No, ma'am. We can't. We'd miss the first act."

The fact that he'd booked the flight only hours before the opera was a scene straight out of *Pretty Woman*. He'd picked her up in a sleek black limousine, and they'd driven down the snowy streets of Marietta, drinking champagne from skinny glasses. She felt more like Julia Roberts than she had a right to.

She leaned her head against his shoulder, and looked out at the hangars, which were trimmed with tiny white lights. They glowed softly through the falling snow—peacefully, joyfully. She felt warm and floaty from the champagne, but mostly, she felt in love. The opera was Jake's Christmas gift to her, but more than that, it had turned out to be the gift of himself. He was giving her something that hadn't come easily, she knew. It was a symbol of change, of the future. And she treasured it with all her heart.

"I feel like you need a dog," she said, as the plane jerked forward, the pilot positioning its nose toward the runway.

He laughed. "That was random."

"You're not on the road anymore, and that's why you said you didn't have one before. Maybe now's the time."

He was quiet for a minute, considering this. "I guess you're right," he said. "No more excuses."

"Buckshot is sweet, but it's not the same."

"No. And he can't be trusted on the carpet."

She grinned. "Nope."

"So...will you come with me to pick this dog out? I wouldn't even know where to start. Big, small. Fluffy, not fluffy. Who the hell knows."

The Cessna's engines hummed in Alice's ears as the plane began taxiing down the runway. The snow was just a blur now, the Christmas lights on the hangars only the sweetest memory. The plane sped down the tarmac, smooth as glass.

It was like ice-skating over Miracle Lake, and when they lifted into the air, the butterflies in her stomach took flight, too.

She squeezed his hand, and he squeezed hers back. She'd never felt so safe as when she was with Jake. "That's the beauty of it," she said. "You just follow your heart."

"Okay. When we end up with a bulldog, Chihuahua mix, I'm blaming you."

She laughed. *We.* Leaning into him, she drew comfort from his warmth. From his solid, steady presence beside her. One little word that was changing everything for her. And she knew she'd never be quite the same again.

The plane climbed, climbed, up into the winter sky, through the snow and clouds. Soon, they'd break through to where the stars glittered and the heavens were as black as an evening gown. It was somewhere she never thought she'd feel at home, thousands of feet above the ground. Holding the hand of a man who made her heart race. But she was learning all kinds of new things about herself. That she was an adventuress, for one. That she had the ability to love a country mile, for another.

And it was the most precious discovery.

The End

Want more? Check out Lucky and Rachel's story in
Christmas at Sleigh Bell Farm!

Join Tule Publishing's newsletter for more great reads and weekly deals

If you enjoyed *Betting on the Bull Rider,*
you'll love the other book in....

The Elliotts of Montana series

Book 1: *Christmas at Sleigh Bell Farm*

Book 2: *Betting on the Bull Rider*

Available now at your favorite online retailer!

More books by Kaylie Newell

The Harlow Brothers series

The Harlow brothers learned at a young age that family is what you make of it. Born on the wrong side of the tracks and abandoned by their father, Judd, Luke and Tanner have grown into remarkably tough men who are jaded by life. But when they come together as guardians of their orphaned half-sister, they'll find that love is what you make of it, too. As they learn how to be the fathers they never had, their carefully constructed walls begin to crack. But it will take three strong women to tear those defenses down for good, and show them what true happiness looks like.

Book 1: *Tanner's Promise*

Book 2: *Luke's Gift*

Book 3: *Judd's Vow*

Available now at your favorite online retailer!

About the Author

For Kaylie Newell, storytelling is in the blood. Growing up the daughter of two gifted writers, she knew eventually she'd want to follow in their footsteps. While she's written short stories her whole life, it wasn't until after her kids were born that she decided to shoot for the moon and write her first romance novel. She hasn't looked back since!

Kaylie lives in Southern Oregon with her husband, two little girls, two indifferent cats and a mutt named Pedro.

Thank you for reading

Betting on the Bull Rider

If you enjoyed this book, you can find more from all our great authors at TulePublishing.com, or from your favorite online retailer.

TULE
PUBLISHING

Made in the USA
Middletown, DE
21 September 2021